STOP SERGIO!

The Visitor from the End of the World

Paul Andrews

**Grosvenor House
Publishing Limited**

The right of Paul Andrews to be identified as the author of this
work has been asserted in accordance with Section 78
of the Copyright, Designs and Patents Act 1988

The book cover picture is copyright to Inmagine Corp LLC

This book is published by
Grosvenor House Publishing Ltd
Link House
140 The Broadway, Tolworth, Surrey, KT6 7HT.
www.grosvenorhousepublishing.co.uk

This book is a work of fiction. Any resemblance to
people or events, past or present, is purely coincidental.

A CIP record for this book
is available from the British Library

ISBN 978-1-78623-408-7

'Stop Mark Robins'

A summary of Paul Andrews' first novel

Josh Stanton, an effervescently friendly young lad from Liverpool, inadvertently found himself back in the year 1989 when stepping into a strange spherical bubble emanating from a derelict house situated near to Anfield, Liverpool FC's football ground.

Trapped in 1989, Josh got to meet his late father for the first time since he was killed in a tragic road accident when Josh was only 5 years old. Together they watched their beloved Liverpool during the 1989-1990 season – one which saw the Anfield men win their last league title and confirm their superiority over their great rivals, Manchester United.

Josh Stanton knew their superiority would not last for much longer. Being the massively avid Liverpool fan that he was, he couldn't resist the urge to meddle with the natural course of football history when stopping Mark Robins score an incredibly important goal. That goal helped lay the platform for an incredibly golden period of success for Manchester United, which saw them surpass Liverpool in winning league titles. It also included a glorious treble in 1999, culminating in them winning the Champions League in dramatic style, with two late goals against Bayern Munich.

Josh was to realise the monumental error of his ways when he finally managed to return to his own time and found himself in a future that was much grimmer than the reality he was supposed to be in. He was to find that his father was still alive but now battling a very cruel and crippling disease, having warned him about his fate in 1998. He was also to find that his best friend no longer existed and that all the previous cordiality of the people he knew had now been replaced with hostility. Worst of all, his beloved Liverpool had now dramatically fallen from grace and their local rivals, Everton, had grown into an incredible trophy-winning powerhouse completely dominating the city. All this had stemmed from Josh's actions in the past. It was obvious that he would have to return to the past once more, to undo all the wrongs he had created and restore the future to the way it should always have been.

It was during the return to the past that Josh Stanton met the gloriously enchanting Emma Chambers. They fell in love, but this was never supposed to happen at that moment in time. Josh knew their romance would be brief, as he knew two versions of himself could not co-exist. Once his natural conception was achieved in 1992, leading to his natural birth in 1993, it meant that his version of himself in the past would just fade from existence and merge back into his embryotic self. Knowing that he was going to disappear, Josh tried to explain everything to Emma but it was too much for her to believe, and she was left heartbroken and full of anguish. Josh left Emma a goodbye letter which he begged her not to tear up as it would confirm in the future that he hadn't been lying to her and would explain how he was living in the year 2010 and enjoying college life.

Back in the present day, all the wrongs of Josh's time travel adventures had seemingly been corrected and everything seemed normal and as it should be. But Josh couldn't help noticing the new attractive lady tutor of English Literature at his college, and that this interest was being reciprocated. The tutor was Emma Chambers – now 18 years older but still enticingly magical. She had kept Josh's letter, against her better judgement but with an irresistible curiosity to know whether this absurd notion put forward in his letter could actually be true. She now knew that Josh hadn't lied to her after all, but she was very troubled now that she knew Josh was for real.

Emma also had a bombshell admission to share with Josh, something he just had to know... She had been pregnant with his baby when Josh disappeared, so he had a son out there who was actually older than he was! A son born outside the natural rules of time! Emma revealed that their son had been adopted, so where was he? How was he?

It was clear that the natural timeline contained a serious flaw. How would everything proceed now?

Prologue

13th May 2012   The Etihad Stadium, Manchester

Quite possibly the most incredible climax to a Premier League season, that will probably never be bettered, as extreme despair gave way to extreme ecstasy among the battle-weary legions of Manchester City fans in the space of a couple of minutes when all seemed hopelessly lost and forlorn.

It was Manchester City v QPR, the last day of an incredibly exciting Premier League season, which had seen Manchester City, the newly-acclaimed 'noisy neighbours', forever exchanging the leadership with their perpetual trophy-laden neighbours, the mighty Manchester United. The followers of Manchester United had relished reminding the loyal City fans of how long it had been since Manchester City had been champions; indeed it had been 44 years.

Manchester City were well known for doing things the hardest possible way. They could always be relied on to make a drama out of a crisis and make their fans suffer in the most tormented way, but surely not today! Not against lowly QPR when there was so much at stake! A win, any win, was all City needed. And all the mercurial talent was at City's disposal.

QPR were fighting for their Premiership lives and would give their all, but surely it was futile against the majestic stardust of Manchester City. The City fans were confident, but you couldn't afford to be too confident when it came to Manchester City. Nothing was ever straightforward, but it would be a football catastrophe if Manchester City didn't win the title now and it resulted in Manchester United wrestling the prize away from them in such cruel, tormenting circumstances. The devastation and magnitude of such a loss would be colossal, and quite possibly one that would be impossible to ever fully get over. The stakes were enormous.

As the match approached its final minute, the unthinkable was reality. Manchester City were 2-1 down to QPR, who had been reduced to 10 men following the sending off of Joey Barton. Attack after frenzied attack was being resisted by a very stubborn QPR defence, and the desperation and forlorn despair was becoming overwhelming. Even when eventually Edin Djeko managed to equalise, it all seemed too little too late. Manchester United had won their game up at Sunderland and were now waiting expectantly on the Sunderland pitch ready to celebrate Manchester City's agony and be crowned champions instead.

Manchester City had one last chance, as good intricate play around QPR's penalty area saw Sergio Aguero in on goal. He still had plenty to do but he sensationally rifled the ball into the net! It was Manchester City 3, QPR 2! A mesmeric eruption of unbridled euphoria filled the Etihad Stadium as the roof was virtually blasted off with the collective, unadulterated joy radiating from every City fan, mixed with the sheer, absolute, desperate relief of it all. The Manchester City fans had been sent to heaven all the way from hell, all thanks to the soul-saving, magic genius of Sergio Aguero. This was how it was meant to be. What if reality had changed?

Josh Stanton was to discover it had, and something was going to happen during this match to dramatically change what was to come and precipitate a heart-breaking journey back to the past for him to save the world from impending doom and restore history to the way it should be. What did Josh have to do? How did the visitor from the end of the world help him? Who was he? And why was he so special? What startling revelations was Josh given by his special visitor, and how did Emma Chambers fit into all this? And what about their son? What did Josh find out about his son? A son born before he was!!

PLEASE READ ON and FIND OUT

Contents

CHAPTER 1

TOO GOOD TO BE TRUE

10th January 2010

It had now been two weeks since Josh last saw Emma Chambers. Manchester College had broken up over Christmas and Emma had used her break to return to visit her parents in Marlow, and to get some much-needed space to come to terms with the unbelievable revelations of the previous college term. Josh Stanton had been wandering around in a stunned daze for the last two weeks, and could not think about anything else than Emma and the tantalising thought that he was a dad.

For Josh, the 10th January couldn't come around quick enough as it was the first day back at Manchester College. He was eager to see Emma again, and to see how she felt and how they could progress their relationship if they could. How would Emma be with him? Josh knew they had a massive amount to discuss, not least whether Emma would be interested in tracing the whereabouts of their adopted son. Where was he? What was his name? What was he like? Josh Stanton knew for certain he was special as he had been born out

1

of the natural timeline to parents of existing timeframes at the time of conception.

Josh was also anxious to confide in and seek advice from his science and physics mentor, Mr Xavier Richardson. Josh was very confident in his prowess and really wanted to have his guidance. The 10ᵗʰ January had seemed like an eternity, but it was now here, and Josh was full of nerves as he approached Emma during the morning break.

"Hi Miss, how are you? Did you have a good break?" Josh asked nervously.

"Yes, I'm fine, Josh. I had a good break and have had time to think about things," answered a reassuringly friendly Emma.

"What have you decided, Emma? How did you see us? Did you tell your folks about me? And did they know anything about me or remember me?" Josh asked, overcome with curiosity.

"I want us to be friends, Josh. I really like you, but all this is so really weird especially as I'm a tutor at your college and I'm twenty years older than you. I do really want us to be friends and see where it takes us. What do you think, Josh?" Emma replied.

"I think that's for the best. as well, I'm glad we can be friends at least. Do your folks remember me?"

"Yes, they actually remember a young lad helping them in the quizzes at our local pub. They liked you, but I couldn't tell them the real reason for your disappearance or they would have been furious. I felt ashamed and scared at being pregnant. I left the area for a short time so I didn't hurt my parents. I felt like I'd really let them down and they didn't deserve that, so I kept my pregnancy from them," Emma answered with candid honesty.

"What made you go through with the pregnancy, Emma? I mean, abortion would have been the easy way out, wouldn't it?" asked a puzzled Josh.

"I loved you, Josh, I really loved you. I didn't believe you would really disappear and be from the future. I always had hope at the time that you'd be back with me so I went ahead with the pregnancy, but it became obvious as time went on that there was no sign of you. So I gave the baby up for adoption as I thought it was for the best, and I didn't want the baby to be a permanent reminder of you as you really, really hurt me."

Emma was becoming overcome with emotion, and Josh could see the hurt in her eyes. He couldn't bear to see her so upset.

"I'm really sorry for whatever I've done. I can't believe I allowed myself to get you in this situation, but I can believe that I did really like you," reassured a heartfelt Josh.

"I know you liked me, Josh, that's what made it all the more difficult. We were blissfully in love. I couldn't accept that you would deliberately hurt me, so I think that's why I kept your letter. For a long time I did hate you, but my heart pulled me round," Emma replied.

Josh and Emma could have talked for ages, but it was time to go their separate ways for the time being as break time was now over. Josh felt reassured about the status of their relationship but hadn't had time to go into more detail about the baby and whether Emma would help him trace the baby. He also wanted to know all about how Emma and how she had lived for the last 20 years. Had she fallen in love with anybody else? All that could wait for another time, but despite his obvious excitement at being a dad, Josh couldn't help having a morbid foreboding at the thought of what it all meant. It should not be possible for this to happen, but now that it had what consequences would have to be faced?

Josh knew the perfect person to confide in was Mr Xavier Richardson, his science and physics mentor.

"Can I have a word with you, sir?" asked a troubled Josh.

"Yes, of course you can, Josh. How can I help you?" Mr Richardson replied.

"Please hear me out, sir, as this is going to sound preposterous, but I think I've created a real problem. Somehow, I have lived in the past, met a girl and fell in love, resulting in an unfortunate pregnancy," an exasperated Josh explained.

"Impossible. Impossible., Impossible! What on earth makes you think that?" a scathingly dismissive Mr Richardson replied.

"I've actually met the person from the past that I fell in love with, and she's now 20 years older than me. I also have a letter in my own handwriting, confirming that I was alive in the past. It's physical evidence I find hard to believe myself, but it's all real," answered Josh.

"How are you supposed to have managed to live in the past?" Mr Richardson continued. "How did you get there in the first place?"

"Apparently I stepped into a strange spherical bubble in a derelict house near Liverpool's football ground," answered Josh. "I also apparently was going to go back to the present day in the same manner." Josh felt so foolish in his explanations, but Mr Xavier Richardson looked very thoughtful.

"I might, just might, have a theory, if what you are telling me has any grain of truth," stated Mr Richardson. "In essence, it is possible you are describing a time bubble. This is supposed to be completely theoretical, but it sounds like you stepped through a time bubble. You shouldn't have been able to penetrate the barrier and it should have repelled you on contact. It could have killed you with its discharge. Do you have anything abnormal about you?" a clearly perplexed Mr Richardson asked.

"I do have AB negative blood which I believe is uncommon," answered Josh.

"There is a possibility that having a certain type of blood could have an earthling type of effect, allowing you to pass through, but like I said, you could have been killed by just touching the barrier. I have an interesting analogy for you," said Mr Richardson.

"I have a funny feeling about what you're going to say, Mr Richardson," Josh replied. "I've got a feeling of *déjà vu* and that you're going to give the egg and the sperm analogy, and that only a tiny particle of sperm penetrates the egg barrier."

"You're right! How did you know I was going to say that?" Mr Richardson asked.

"I know it sounds funny, but in my sub-conscious mind I've heard you telling me this before."

"My goodness, how strange, but I'm getting to believe you more as we go on. This is getting very strange." Mr Richardson was becoming more convinced Josh was somehow telling him the truth, however implausible.

"What do you think could cause this time bubble, sir?" Josh asked.

"It's supposed to be completely theoretical and virtually impossible, but what you are describing is a very concentrated area of distorted time that has somehow made it into our reality of existence. In essence, it is like a blister that has formed onto the fabric of time like you would get a blister on your finger if it was constantly suffering friction with another object. A blister can form due to abnormal friction. You know what a blister represents, don't you, Josh?"

"Er, no, not really," Josh replied, a puzzled look on his face.

"It represents imperfection. Imagine a clean surface, perfectly pristine, but then bubble-like blisters appear on it which makes the surface imperfect. The whole appearance of a time bubble represents imperfection in the natural timeline. You know what blisters can do, don't you, Josh?"

"Pop or burst," Josh answered in horror.

"Let me give you a further analogy, of a car windscreen that's fully intact. This represents the natural timeline and then—"

"I know what you're going to say, sir. I somehow remember hearing you say this before. You're going to say that any imperfection on the windscreen will eventually lead to a crack, with lots of different splinters emanating from this crack, and the whole windscreen can shatter into thousands of pieces. All this, from just a small imperfection, can lead to a calamitous shattering of the whole windscreen."

"Oh, my goodness, if you can remember me telling you this, you must have met me in the past. I must have had a reason to be answering a question from you, and you must have been troubled that you had done something to cause an imperfection. You could well be the cause of this time bubble, and unless it can be corrected the whole natural timeline will shatter at some point in the future. This is absolutely going to happen, unless somehow you can go back and reset the timeline to a point prior to this imperfection forming and getting hold. Otherwise, a temporal explosion is absolutely inevitable; a shattering of the whole timeline a paradox."

Josh Stanton was horror-struck at what he was hearing, that somehow, he could be responsible for a future paradox. How on earth could he put this right? Josh knew from his conversations with Emma that this time bubble was due to appear in July, if what she remembered was correct, and it would appear in a derelict house near Liverpool's Anfield Stadium.

Should Josh go and seek out this bubble and re-enter the past? What if, in doing so, he was going to make a bad problem worse and create even more damage? But what if Josh chose to ignore going back, hoping that everything would be alright and that the natural timeline could be healed or at least the cracks metaphorically papered over? Mr Xavier Richardson's final retort left him in no doubt about what he thought.

"From what you have told me about falling in love and getting her pregnant, I am in no doubt it is you that has caused this imperfection. You are responsible for all this."

"What would happen if I never went back to the past? Wouldn't it mean I never met this lady in 1990, meaning I couldn't get her pregnant, so not harming the future? Wouldn't that be the sensible thing to do? Wouldn't it see a natural erasing of this imperfect history? Wouldn't it lead to the restoration of the natural timeline?" questioned Josh.

"There's one massive imponderable in all this. You made a baby, born out of the natural timeline – a baby that's supposed to not exist! This baby has lived or been affecting lives ever since. The natural erasure might not affect this baby, as normal rules of time might not apply to a person born out of the natural time order. Are you going to tell me who your lady is, so I can talk to her?"

"I'd rather not at this moment as I need to talk to her more, but I will tell you in due course," Josh replied.

"Ok, but I think this lady of yours could well hold the key. I really think you have to go back to the past if you can and effect it from there. That is the answer. This baby must not be born in the first place; it is imperative, absolutely imperative!"

Josh had been left with massive food for thought as he left his meeting with Mr Xavier Richardson. He could feel his feelings for Emma Chambers growing with every moment again, and he was extremely curious to know more about his son, but at the same time it was going to lead to disaster at some point for everybody. Josh would love to "live the moment" but life was not that simple, it was much more complicated. He knew he was going to have to go and seek out this time bubble and take his chances in the past to try and correct things, but would his heart get in the way again? Would he be unable to resist the unmistakable chemistry that he and Emma had?

Josh knew it was a battle his head had to win, but in the meantime, there were a few months in the present day to enjoy, a little longer to learn more about Emma and enjoy her company.

APRIL 2010

Three more months had elapsed, and Josh and Emma were enjoying the best of friendships. Josh still hadn't disclosed to Mr Richardson that it was Emma who had been his special lady in the past.

Everything at Manchester College was perfectly discreet and orderly. There was no impropriety, just a pleasant and respectful way between them, but Josh could tell there was a growing connection which was becoming ever stronger. He could feel it, really feel it, but Josh knew that it could well be short-lived as his predicted rendezvous with this scary time bubble was only a short few weeks away and then this satisfying ease of the present would give way to uncertainty.

As Josh approached his seventeenth birthday, he was delighted to get a gift from Emma. "I hope you like this friendship ring, Josh. I hope it will always remind you of me. Happy Birthday," she said.

"Thank you so much, Emma, I'll treasure it. It means a great deal to me that you have given me this," Josh replied.

"I've also written you this letter," she said. "I know you've wanted to know how I've lived my life during these twenty years and how I felt. I now feel comfortable enough with our friendship to let you see this letter, and I think it'll explain a lot. Here you are, read it later." Josh couldn't wait to find out what it said, but he waited until he got home before opening the letter...

Dear Josh,

This is a letter I thought I'd never get to write, as I thought I'd never see you again, but I never gave up hope that I would. You'll never believe how much you hurt me when you disappeared. It's more than you'll ever know. You were my true love. I was truly in love with you and nobody has come close to the feelings I had for you. I did have a brief fling with this guy, Richard, but very quickly came to realise it wasn't right. The sad truth is that I never got over your disappearance.

I've often wondered how different my life would have been if you hadn't walked into my world all those years ago. Please don't get me wrong, but maybe it would have been kinder for me if you hadn't. It is incredibly hard to ignore true love, so you were irresistible. You left an indelible mark on me which has affected me ever since. The adoption of our baby was very traumatic, but I couldn't cope emotionally, and I thought Josh Junior (as I called him) would be happier with a loving set of adopted parents.

I believe they were coming from Cornwall, so Josh Junior would have a nice life by the sea. It was for the best, but I did this with a very heavy heart.

I don't know how our new friendship will develop in time, but I do know you are very special and always will be.

Yours lovingly,

Emma x

Josh's heart swelled with emotion as he read her words. It confirmed how special a person Emma was, and Josh fervently hoped that she would forever be part of his life. He was also glad to learn a little more about his son, but now it was crystal clear that Josh didn't want to explore this situation as it would become far too emotionally complicated to go ahead with his return to the past and correct all the wrong resetting the past. If he had grown the natural emotional attachment of a father, resetting the past properly would mean making sure his son was never born. It had to be this way, so Josh didn't want to be fully exposed to the intense emotional pain he would face if he could visualise in crystal clarity the person, his own flesh and blood, that he was helping to eradicate from time.

July 1st, 2010

Time Bubble Day

July 1st, 2010 was now approaching with indecent haste. Josh Stanton really didn't want that day to come, as everything was fine in his world and nothing seemed out of place. Did he really have to leave this reality behind? Josh was loving the exquisitely delightful ray of beautiful sunshine that Emma Chambers brought to his world. He had never been so happy!

Football and his beloved Liverpool FC had now been relegated to second place in importance, such was his all-encompassing enchantment with the wonderful Emma. Football had actually become a very distant second to Emma, so much so that for the first time ever, Josh had ignored what was for every football fan the equivalent of waking up on Christmas morning — Fixtures Day!!! The day filled with the excitement of seeing who Liverpool were going to play and when, all the planning of future trips and the intoxicating anticipation of these trips. Fixtures Day had always provided Josh with a massive adrenalin rush, but this year it had just passed over him.

Josh certainly did seem to be love struck again. The poor lad certainly had it bad. Did it really all have to end? What if he could never find this level of happiness again?

When July 1st arrived, Josh had a really heavy heart when he saw Emma Stanton for the last time. Would he ever see her again? Lots of things could go wrong, far too many to mention, so Josh tried not to think about it or it would drive him crazy. He had dared not mention to Emma what he was about to do, as it just wasn't fair on her to be put through the emotional rollercoaster once again. If everything went to plan, then hopefully she would never need to know or even be aware of anything different; it was the best way! It was best for everyone.

The one-person Josh wanted by his side when confronting the bubble would be his tutor, Mr Xavier Richardson. Josh needed all the help he could get, and who better than his very knowledgeable tutor who had also become by now a very good confidant? Josh could trust Mr Richardson implicitly and he loved the older man's openness. In fact, perhaps the only thing Josh didn't particularly like was the analogies!

"Are you ready, sir? I'm really nervous," said an anguished Josh as they approached the boarded-up houses near Anfield Stadium.

"I won't lie to you, Josh," Mr Richardson replied, "you should be very nervous, as there is so much that can go wrong. It just has to be done or we're all doomed in the future, so you have to get this right this time."

"Thanks for that, sir," Josh replied with mock sincerity.

"Which house did you think you went into, Josh?" asked Mr Richardson.

"I believe it was the last house in the street," replied Josh. "It's my strong feeling of *déjà vu* that it was the last house on the street. I remember having the feeling of being distracted by an emanating glow from inside the house and exploring what it was."

"Well, I hate to say this, but look all around you. There's no sign of any glowing light anywhere. Are you sure you've got the right day?" a troubled Mr Richardson asked.

"All my feelings of *déjà vu* have been right up until now. The time bubble should be here, something is not right," protested a disbelieving Josh.

"I believe you, Josh, but something bad has really happened. It means the time dynamic has changed and altered, so you won't be able to correct anything anytime soon. We're all in the unknown territory now, God help us all! Maybe the fact that the bubble isn't here now is not the end of it. It might appear at a different, better time."

"We were dealing with a lot of guesswork in determining how and when I should re-appear in the past. Everything needs to be precise, so maybe this is a blessing in disguise. You know the saying, don't you, sir? 'Everything happens for a reason.'" Josh was trying hard to put a positive spin on things.

"Ten out of ten for trying to be optimistic, but you haven't realised something, Josh. Do you remember our conversation when you asked me about not going in the bubble?" asked Mr Richardson.

"Yes," replied Josh.

"Well, I did say that there was a massive imponderable as to why that wasn't an option, and time couldn't just correct itself and erase the imperfection. It's because of the birth of your son. It was an unnatural birth out of the natural timeline, an imperfection that just can't be naturally erased unless it's stopped at source. I'm in no doubt you expected to see this time bubble, but all the time dynamics have already changed and it's all down to this child. It is confirmation that the world is in trouble, and I don't know if it can be undone now." Mr Richardson was very pessimistic in his outlook.

"Let me give you an analogy," he went on. "Imagine time is like a bone in your body and is fine until something happens and causes your bone to break and you suffer a fracture. What do you do, Josh?"

"You obviously get it seen to, have it plastered, and allow it to re-heal," Josh answered.

"Yes, and usually the break heals eventually, leading to your bone being perfectly fine again so there's no problem. But what if your bone isn't mending properly? What would happen if your bone was mending in a completely unnatural way and was healing in a different angle to how it should?"

"You'd be in agony, so you would need to have the bone re-broken and reset for it to try and mend properly," answered Josh, registering the point Mr Richardson was making.

"Exactly! What I am metaphorically trying to say is that time in agony, because it's mending all wrong and needs to be re-broken for it to have a chance to recover properly. The break needs to be clean through with no compound complication. That is time's only hope. It's our only hope!" Mr Richardson was typically forthright. "You can see why I'm troubled, can't you, Josh?"

Josh was equally very troubled, but there was very little he could do now. It was time to go back to Manchester, but there he could at least find an enjoyable solace in the delightful shape of Emma Chambers, and time travel could wait for another time – pardon the pun.

As Josh Stanton and Xavier Richardson arrived back in Manchester, there was going to be a very rude awakening for Josh as the full implications of the time bubble's failure to appear would become fully evident. What was Josh going to discover?

CHAPTER 2

DAWN OF UNCERTAINTY

(Uncertainty breeds speculation and speculation
breeds uncertainty)

July 2010

It wasn't going to take long for Josh Stanton's world to
come crashing down from the blissful era of happiness
he'd been experiencing. Josh hadn't told Emma of his
aborted trip to Liverpool, but when he tried to contact
her on her mobile phone he was puzzled to get an "I'm
sorry but this number is not recognised, please hang
up" message. Josh was confused and dumbfounded.
Three more efforts got the same response.

What's going on? This is weird, thought an unsettled Josh.
He couldn't wait to see Emma at college the next day to
see what was happening. But why couldn't he contact her?

Arriving at Manchester College the following morning
shattered any illusions Josh had that there was a perfectly
reasonable explanation. He made his way to the English
Literature section of the campus to see Emma but was

met by a ferociously feisty middle-aged lady tutor, who definitely wasn't Miss Emma Chambers. Her tone wasn't exactly friendly either.

"Can I help you? Aren't you supposed to be somewhere else? Move on, you're not supposed to be in here." The woman's tone was devoid of any warmth.

Josh didn't want to stick around, but he needed to know something. "I'm very sorry to disturb you, Miss, but can you tell me where Miss Chambers is, please?" a nervous Josh asked.

"Who on earth is Miss Chambers? There is no-one here of that name. Now, please be on your way," was her cold reply.

What on earth is happening? mused an exasperated Josh. *This is unbelievable, terrible. Where is she?* Josh's head was all over the place as he walked around the college in a complete daze. Nobody had ever heard of a Miss Emma Chambers, was Josh going totally mad? Was Emma just a figment of imagination in Josh's mind?

As Josh gazed down at the middle finger of his left hand, the mystery deepened further. Sitting proudly on this finger was the friendship ring Emma had given him for his birthday. The ring hadn't disappeared or been eradicated, but the person who gave him the ring seemed to have disappeared or, even worse, been eradicated.

What about Emma's letter? thought Josh. *Is it still in my drawer?* Josh proceeded to open his top drawer, and there it was! The letter was there in all its glory, so he wasn't going mad after all. But something was very wrong! There was only one person he could turn to and that was Mr Xavier Richardson; he was the only person who could understand. Mr Richardson had been with him during his aborted Liverpool trip, and was the only person who could make sense of things.

"Sir, Sir, something's gone badly wrong!"

"Calm down, Josh. Take a deep breath and tell me what's wrong."

"Miss Emma Chambers has disappeared, and no-one's ever seen or heard of her. It's like she's never been here. Do you remember Emma, sir?" Josh replied anxiously.

"Of course, I know Miss Chambers. She's the tutor of English Literature. She's a lovely lady," answered Mr Richardson.

"Well, she's disappeared, and you're the first and only person that can remember her, apart from me," Josh said, having great difficulty in controlling his anguish.

"My goodness! How unbelievable! I'm afraid I was worried this was going to get very crazy. Do you have anything you need to tell me, Josh?" Mr Richardson had clearly sensed there were some details Josh was withholding from him.

"Yes, sir. Emma Chambers was the special lady in question. When I was talking to you earlier, I didn't want to tell you as I felt very uncomfortable and I didn't know how you would feel about it as she was a tutor at the college. It was very awkward, but I have to tell you everything now as I don't know what's happened to her or what to do. I badly need your help, sir," a very emotional Josh replied.

"Well, well, well! So, she was the lady in question, was she? I kind of sensed that she might be, as whenever I saw her talking to you, I just couldn't help noticing the unmistakable chemistry between you both. It did make me wonder! It looked like you were floating on air. I'm afraid I'm beginning to realise what has happened," countered a forthright Mr Richardson.

"Please tell me, sir. I'm very worried," pleaded Josh.

"Reality has changed, but in a subtle way. Remember, you were expecting to go back in time, but couldn't do so as you previously did. So, in theory, how could you have met Emma Chambers in 1990? And why did she have any reason to be at Manchester College in the present day?" Mr Richardson answered.

"Please look at my middle finger, sir. That's a friendship ring – a ring given to me by Emma just three months ago. Shouldn't that have erased or no longer be here? I also still have a letter from her in my drawer, and that hasn't erased either. She was really here until yesterday. You can remember her, yet nobody else has ever heard of her. This is all weird, it doesn't make sense." Josh was now filling up with emotion.

"I do think I have an explanation or theory. Have a look at what I'm going to show you, Josh," Mr Richardson said as he proceeded to draw some diagrams on a piece of paper.

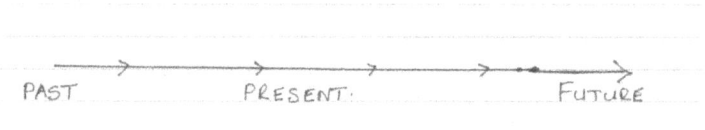

"This line represents the natural timeline, Josh. A perfectly straight line with no interference, that's how it should be. Now let me draw you this.

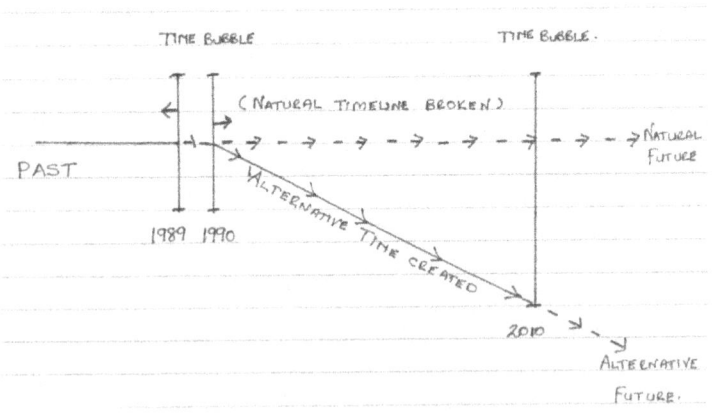

"From what you have told me when you first went back in time, this is what I understand has happened. You can see that what you did in the past disturbed the natural timeline, forcing it to spear off into a tangent, getting ever wider as time moves on, resulting in you experiencing a vastly different alternative future

22

reality," Mr Richardson explained, now fully in his element.

"That's all well and good, sir, but what about now and what is happening now? How do you explain what's going on now, sir?" Josh asked.

"Let me draw you this, Josh. This is what I suspect has happened and it's not great. I think we're all in a lot of trouble. Remember you told me that you caused a pregnancy? You have a baby that was born outside the natural rules of time, and now you've missed the chance to correct the wrongs of the past. I believe you will find that this baby still exists or existed. I believe you'll find that this baby wasn't eradicated and is now probably 18 years old and living just as much as we are. When you missed the time bubble, all the rules of eradication couldn't be fully implemented, and time couldn't be naturally reset. In essence, the birth of your baby represents a 'foreign body' in the system, an imperfection that has caused a massive problem.

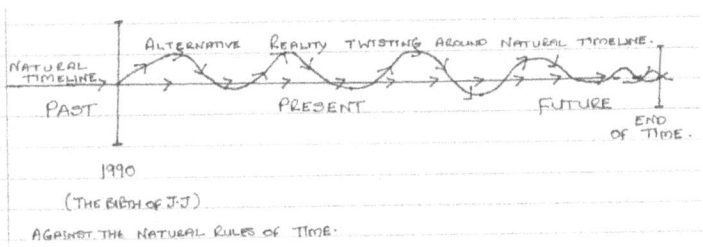

"What I believe is that time has become twisted and tangled. There is a temporal overlay, which would explain how we can remember Emma and the physical evidence remains when it shouldn't. Emma is now probably living a totally different existence, oblivious to knowing anything about you. Different realities have become entangled and wrapped around each other, causing a great amount of friction. As they intersect, this friction will eventually cause a paradox. As it becomes too great, basically somewhere down the line in the future, time will explode. It will be the end of time, the end of the world."

It was all very doom-laden stuff that Mr Richardson was saying, and there was no respite as he continued, "I think the fact that time has become entangled is the reason you never got to see the time bubble when you should have. The mechanics of twisted time or twisted realities would have greatly inhibited the potential that a bubble could form and remain stable. Unless somehow someone can find a way to induce a time bubble so that you can go back to the past before time becomes entangled with different realities, then I'm afraid we're all doomed. It's just a question of when."

"Why are you so confident that Emma's baby would be unaffected by the bubble not appearing and still be fully alive as a teenager today?" Josh asked.

"I believe the fact he was born outside the natural rules of time would be in a temporal air pocket. You know the trouble air pockets can bring, don't you, Josh?"

"I suppose so, sir, but what are you trying to tell me?" replied a puzzled Josh.

"Let me give you analogy."

"Oh sir, do you have to?" Josh replied, knowing how keen Mr Richardson was to deal in analogies, but they could be very unorthodox.

"Imagine for a moment that time is a radiator and it's all lovely, warm, and fully operational. Then all of a sudden, an air pocket develops in the system, the radiator stops functioning properly, and large areas become increasingly cold, devoid of any heat at all. It's all down to that air pocket, and that's the damage air pockets can do. I think you have caused your very own air pocket – a temporal air pocket which is causing time to break down. What we must do is bleed the time radiator and get rid of the air pocket, but of course it's not that simple. The pocket must be stopped before it forms in the first place, as it's already caused damage to the time radiator. I'm sorry to be blunt, as you have a son but he shouldn't exist, and the very presence of your son has put all future mankind in massive danger. It would have been so much easier if the bubble hadn't collapsed and you could have gone back and prevented his birth. But now he's alive and out there, are you going to try and find him? It's going to make things extremely difficult for you, should a way be found to get you back to the past. What are you going to do, Josh?"

That was a very good question! Josh was naturally very curious about his son, but his priority for now was to find out more about what has happened to Emma Chambers. Where was she? How was she? Would Emma even know who Josh was anymore? Josh had to know for his own sanity. Emma meant everything to him; she was Josh's world, and all he could think about was Emma. She was the centre of his every thought, and Josh was heartbroken at the thought that she had gone.

Josh was crestfallen. Manchester College was due to break up for summer recess, so it was time to visit to Emma's home town to see if he could get any answers and any respite from this twisting reality.

AUGUST 2010

Josh was full of nervous anticipation as he approached Marlow, Emma Chambers' home town. Josh had never visited the place, but his mind was full of images of the town. The sense of *déjà vu* in his mind was overwhelming. It was almost like he had an encyclopaedic knowledge of where he was going.

On arrival in Marlow, all these images were confirmed. Josh was on sensual overdrive as he walked by the River Thames, strolled past people picnicking in the park, walked under the chain bridge towards Marlow weir, and on to a place where he felt intense emotion as he surveyed the sight of Marlow Locks and the benches that overlooked it. Goose pimples were extending all over his body as he could sense this was where he had spent special romantic times with Emma. This feeling was overwhelming but beautiful, and it brought home the urgent need within him to try and see Emma again.

Josh moved on to the Wycombe Road area of the town, where he hoped to meet some people that knew Emma.

He believed it was his best hope of some answers. The sight of the pub on the corner of Wycombe Road brought more vivid images into Josh's mind, urging him to go in and investigate. He had a strong sense that perhaps Emma had worked there. Was she actually working there now?

The board outside was advertising quizzes, which also struck a chord with Josh as he proceeded to enter the pub. Inside, he nervously surveyed all around in the hope of finding any comforting evidence that Emma was present or nearby, but alas there was no definite comfort to be had. It was time to grasp the nettle and ask someone if they had seen or even heard of her. The landlord would be the best person to ask, as he would know all the regulars.

Josh took a massive intake of breath as he approached the bar. "I'll have an orange juice and a packet of crisps, please." Josh braced himself to ask the important question.

"That'll be £2.10, please," said the landlord.

"Thank you." Josh handed over the coins. "I hope I'm not bothering you but I'm looking for an Emma Chambers, does she come in here?" he asked, his heart racing at a tremendous pace.

It seemed like an eternity before the landlord responded, but it was going to be the first major breakthrough in Josh's search. "Oh, I remember Emma, she used to work here for us as a barmaid until she moved away."

Josh's heart sunk like a stone, but he needed to know more. "Do you know where she went?"

The landlord frowned. "Why are you asking? Do you know her?" The man was clearly not keen to carelessly divulge information to somebody he'd just met.

"She was a good friend of my father, who used to come in here. We're from up north and I wanted to catch up with her to see how she is. I'm Josh Stanton, by the way." He smiled, hoping to resonate a friendly persona, at the same time being careful not to disclose that it was actually he who was her friend as it would sound unbelievable.

"Emma hasn't worked here for a few years," the landlord replied. "Her parents still come in occasionally and tell me how she's doing. I think they are the best people to ask, as the last I heard I think she was very unhappy. The parents never wanted her to get involved with that Richard guy in the first place, but she was headstrong and didn't listen. When Richard came in here, I was always having to tell him to watch the amount he was drinking. He did have this menacing way about him." The man looked thoughtful before going on. "I think they are living together in London, as far as I know. Was your father a friend of Michael's?"

Josh wasn't sure who Michael was, but again there was a strange feeling of being aware of a person named Michael in Emma's past. He feigned a degree of recognition in his response so as not to betray the landlord's belief that Josh was a friend to Emma in this reality. "I wouldn't say he was a close friend, but I think he knew him vaguely. Why do you ask?" Josh asked, full of curiosity.

"Michael is a great lad. I always thought they were meant to be together as they were childhood sweethearts. He was by far the best boyfriend she'd had, as all the others were right idiots in my opinion. It's such a shame that it didn't work out. I know he wanted her back; he even broke off his engagement, but she was smitten by this new customer we had in.

"That sounds like your dad, he was from the north like you. He helped her parents in the quizzes we have here, but he just disappeared and stopped coming. He must have gone back up north." The landlord looked more closely at Josh. "Come to think of it, you're quite similar in looks, if I remember right, so I'm not surprised your dad is a friend of Emma's. Would you like her parents' address?" He seemed to sense that Josh would've been a welcome friend in Emma's world, albeit he didn't know how special.

"Yes, please, I would be most grateful if you could," Josh answered.

Josh now had to decide the best way to approach Emma's parents, knowing that they might be wary of someone they probably didn't recognise and who was so young. They might be reluctant to enlighten Josh in his quest to know more about Emma's world, but his earnest heart yearned to see her again if at all possible. He thought long and hard, and realised he wanted to write a letter for her parents to pass onto her once he had got their trust.

It was his best hope in this new uncertain world, so he proceeded to write down his thoughts.

It felt surreal to bear his soul to a person who had probably never heard of or seen him before. All Josh could hope for was that Emma would have the same extraordinary senses of perception that he possessed and entertain the idea that somehow she did indeed know Josh albeit in a different reality. Josh proceeded with his letter.

Dear Emma,

My name is Josh Stanton and, please don't be alarmed, I believe I'm an old friend of yours and want to get in touch with you again or at least know how you are. I can prove if you allow me that I am a really good friend of yours. It would be great to meet you and catch up. If my name doesn't mean anything to you, I can understand you wondering what this is all about, but please believe me, please trust your gut instinct. I hope you will let your parents know if you are open to getting in touch. I will leave them my contact details.

Yours faithfully,

Josh Stanton

Josh duly called on Emma's parents and was pleasantly surprised at how welcoming they were, considering they must have felt he was a total stranger. Once again, though, there must have been an instinctual trust and belief that everything Josh was telling them about being an acquaintance of Emma's was correct. Her parents agreed to pass on Josh's letter, but explained that Emma's partner, Richard, was very jealous and possessive, even potentially abusive, so everything would have to be very discreet. However, they were willing to pass the letter on to her at the right opportunity.

Josh was very grateful to Mr and Mrs Chambers but was now concerned and alarmed about Emma's welfare. The fact that she was in a relationship, however seemingly flawed, was a dagger in Josh's heart. All he could do was wait and see if Emma responded. Josh had found out a lot from his mission in Marlow, and it was now time to return to his life in Manchester and Liverpool. He knew he had to move on with his life and somehow maybe, just maybe, try to accept that Emma Chambers would no longer be in his life.

It was not in his hands, so Josh had to concentrate on other matters, including the not inconsequential problem that the future was flawed and was leading to the end of the world, due to the timeline being twisted around different realities. Somehow there must be a way for Josh to return to the past, if the world had any hope. There was also the extremely intriguing thought that he had a son.

Josh needed to keep his mind busy for his own sanity; if it was empty, the searing pain of knowing Emma was literally history would be eternally tormenting for him. Hope was now the ultimate byword in Josh's world

– hope that the world could be saved, and hope that Emma would make contact. Hope was all Josh had!

As he headed back to his home in Liverpool, he knew his world might never be the same again. How long, if at all, would it before contact would be made by Emma? Could it be possible that Emma would take Josh's letter seriously, or would she just dismiss it as fantasy-driven rubbish?

CHAPTER 3

THERE'S SOMETHING ABOUT J.J. (JOSH JUNIOR)

DECEMBER 2010

It was now approaching Christmas – four months since Josh's summer trip to Marlow – and the sense of resignation in his heart was growing ever bigger as time moved on. There had been not a sign of any contact or attempted contact from Emma or her parents; it was not looking promising at all!

Josh certainly didn't feel like celebrating Christmas. It can be a magical time for lots of people, but when things are not right Christmas could be the worst times. And that was the case for Josh. He wasn't even enjoying his football as his mind was forever distracted and thinking about this wonderful lady who was no longer around and had obviously moved on with her life, albeit in a twisting reality. It is massively difficult to pour your heart out in a leap of faith, only to find that the object of your affections doesn't respond or reciprocate when you've dared yourself to believe that she would.

It is shattering to a person's belief and confidence, and that was how Josh was now feeling. He felt like the true Grinch of Christmas, but by the New Year Josh was determined to completely refresh his thoughts. He absolutely had to, or he would go mad.

Josh had to immerse himself in other pursuits to keep his mind totally busy and hope that would be enough to offset the heartache he was suffering. He had to set goals, even though he had been warned not to try and find his son as it would make a future trip to the past (pardon the paradox!) all the more emotionally difficult, if not impossible, if he had to implement an action that would see his son never exist in the first place. It was the way it had to be! But Josh had made up his mind that he wanted to find his son, as he was naturally interested in him. His insatiable curiosity about his son would be a welcome antidote to the heartache he was suffering at his perceived rejection from Emma.

He would have to take a chance that if he discovered his son, it was very possible there would never be a way to return to the past. If that was the case, Josh might as well try and enjoy the present, and the best way to enjoy that was to spend it in the company of his son – especially now that the prospect of true love was elusive. Josh had to maximise the present knowing the future was bleak, so he knew he had to snap out his despondency. Life was literally too short not to; the future could finish instantaneously at any point!

It was definitely a case of New Year, new year! But Josh would have to create the illusion he was acting on behalf of his own father, because the person he was searching for was the same age as Josh was. So, he couldn't dare say that *he* was the father.

JANUARY 2011

As the year began, Josh Stanton poured his heart and soul into online searching. He didn't have much to go on, but he was determined to leave no stone unturned in his search. All Josh knew so far was that Emma had said she had been pregnant at Josh's return to the future during their relationship. But it must have been at the early stages as there was no obvious sign that Emma was pregnant when Josh had to return to the future, or at least was trying to when he faded into his embryonic self – and that was July 1992. Josh could target his search to late February-early March 1993 for the day of the child's birth.

Josh also knew Emma had decided to call the baby Josh, after him, so he had a name to type in and a time period; it was a start. He wasn't daring to expect too much from his initial search but as he typed in the name… Josh Chambers, and refined the year search to early 1993, and restricted the search to the home counties region, with the added bonus of adding mother's name as Emma Chambers… there was an instant response. An instant confirmation of Josh Stanton's son's birth certificate was there in black and white.

Josh's gaze was transfixed at the confirmation of it all. His search had borne fruit already, and now he had to capitalise on this and find out where in Cornwall Josh's adopted parents lived and if they were still there now. Emma had said in her letter that the adopted parents were coming from Cornwall, so Josh would have a nice life by the sea. Josh had a shortlist of places that fitted that criteria the best, and suspected that it could well be Newquay, St Ives, Falmouth, Bude, or Penzance. But in truth it could be anywhere, as Cornwall had miles and miles of coastline.

Determined to try and find his son, Josh was prepared to invest in a private investigator if he had to, as he knew the process could take a very long time. And with his own name not being on the certificate as the father, it would be very troublesome to get official help – if not impossible.

Josh wanted to know about Josh Junior as soon as possible and couldn't help having dreams about showing his son his beloved Anfield, watching Liverpool play. Lots of thoughts entered Josh's head: *I wonder who Josh Junior supports? Does he even like football? What does he look like? Will he sue me if he has my looks? Has he got a girlfriend? Is she pretty? Most importantly, is he healthy? And if I get to meet him, will we form a good bond?* Josh had lots of questions he wanted to know the answers to, so the irresistible urge to invest in an investigator was too hard to ignore. The process was initiated with immediate haste, though Josh had to give the impression that he was engaging the investigator on behalf of his ill dad, to avoid arousing suspicion about the absurdity of his situation.

JULY 2011

Josh Stanton was becoming more and more impatient as summer arrived and there had still been no concrete news. It was driving Josh mad that all his efforts seemed to have come to nothing. Josh had still never heard back from Emma's parents, or Emma herself, and that had now been a full year. Life was extremely frustrating in Josh's world, and his beloved Liverpool had just finished another underwhelming season. He was truly in a state of flux!

He looked down at his middle finger and Emma's friendship ring and reflected deeply on the futility of still wearing it. It was starting to symbolise emptiness, a paradise lost, and he was tempted to remove it to allow himself to move on. When you've seemingly lost true love, or something special, the last thing you want is a constant reminder of it. Instead, you have to try and retune your mind to positive alternatives or have a hope to aim for, so the temptation was great. But something inside Josh's mind was urging him to refrain, an instinct from deep inside his soul.

Josh was suddenly presented with a major distraction, with a call from his investigating service. They had news – at last! Josh could feast on some adrenalin as he made his way to a long-awaited appointment with the investigator. His heart was pumping to the maximum as he entered the building. What would they tell him about JJ (Josh Junior)?

Josh Stanton's eyes were transfixed on the piece of paper he was given. The investigators had done a lot of valuable work for him. All the golden nuggets of information were contained on this document: Josh James Chambers, a healthy young baby boy, given up for adoption to a Mr and Mrs Murphy of The Rock, Newquay, Cornwall in April 1993...

That's a good start. I've been to Newquay a few times, so I know it quite well, Josh pondered positively. He studied the paper further as it went on to explain, 'Upon discreet enquiries in the town, we have managed to ascertain that Josh was a very popular boy. In fact, he was infectiously joyful and pleasant to be around, and everybody seemed to like him at his junior school. He had lots of friends. He is tall (like you), has fair hair, and was good at sports, especially football. He regularly made all the school football teams, so physically was in good health.'

Josh looked up from reading the document and smiled. "This sounds great. Good lad! My father will be very happy to know this."

The investigator replied, "He will be especially interested to know that we have made discreet contact with the adopted parents, trying to ascertain whether they would entertain the idea of you being able to meet them to discuss Josh Junior, on your father's behalf, as there are things that he needs to know which are best coming from them. And they are prepared to do this. We must advise you that Josh Junior, as you like to refer him, is no longer living with his adopted parents, and as far as we know he doesn't even still live in Newquay. The adopted parents no longer know where he is, but they are anxious for you to see them on your dad's behalf. Are you prepared to go down and talk to them?"

"Yes, of course," replied a very concerned Josh. "I wonder what they need to tell me."

"As I said, it's best that they get the chance to tell you in person. We have an idea that it's more appropriate to see them, so you can relay everything to your father."

At that, Josh thanked and paid the investigator for his efforts. It was now down to Josh to travel down to Cornwall to see Mr and Mrs Murphy and find out why they were anxious to talk to him. What on earth couldn't be sent to him without Josh seeing them? He was very worried, but it was July and the thought of spending some quality time in the wonderful surfing mecca of Newquay in the middle of summer was very appealing. It would also give Josh a good sense of the environment in which Josh Junior had grown up.

As Josh made his way down to Newquay, he realised that he was potentially opening up a massive can of worms and going against the advice of his now good friend Mr Xavier Richardson. But he had now developed an insatiable curiosity and wanted to see it through as he'd already gone so far. Gone too far might be the description he was feeling as he approached the wonderful location of The Rock in Newquay.

"Wow, what a stunning place to live!" exclaimed Josh as he surveyed the majestic position The Rock enjoyed, surrounded by the ragingly powerful North Atlantic, the waves smashing ferociously onto its rocks below. It was as though the house had its very own island, with its only lifeline a bridge connecting to the mainland on the right-hand side, and on the left it was at the mercy of the ocean. Josh was in total awe as he crossed the bridge and braced himself for an emotional and possibly traumatic encounter. Was he ready for what Mr and Mrs Murphy had to tell him?

Josh rang the doorbell and waited nervously for the door to open. But he was calmed by the welcoming reception he received from a mature and respectable looking couple who greeted him at the door.

"Hello, you must be Josh Stanton's son," said a warm and friendly Mr Murphy. "Please come in and make yourself at home. You both share the same name, don't you? I'm sorry that your father is unwell and can't come to see us in person, but I'm sure that you will pass onto him everything we can tell you. It is very important."

"I certainly will. I can assure you he will know everything that you tell me," Josh told them.

"That's good to hear. I must say we are thrilled to meet you, as you must be a half-brother to our Josh, aren't you?" the man went on.

"I guess so," answered Josh, knowing he was so much more than that.

"It's obvious that you are related, as you look so much like him, at least until he started…" an anguished Mrs Murphy began. "Does your father look like you?"

40

"Absolutely. We have an uncanny resemblance," Josh replied.

"I hope we will get to meet him when he's better. Can you please send him our regards and tell him he's welcome to meet us. If you are any guide, then I'm sure he must be a good dad," she added.

"Thank you. You've got a fantastic place here, it's absolutely awesome!" replied Josh.

"That's nice of you to say so, Josh. We are very lucky, but we have worked very hard for this. It's good, although when it's high tide the sea can be very noisy and the winds can get scary. It can keep you awake at night, but you get used to it." She smiled.

"It's a wonderful place for a boy to grow up in. Did Josh really like it?" asked Josh.

"Oh yes, he absolutely loved it! Josh was very proud to live here, he'd always bring his friends from school to impress them. I presume you'd like to know all about him, wouldn't you?" asked Mr Murphy, knowing full well that was why Josh was there.

"Yes, please. I'm keen to know what you can tell me," replied a very grateful Josh. "I'll pass it on to my father."

"He will be pleased to know Josh (junior) was an absolutely wonderful son; you couldn't wish for a better son. He was fantastically cute with a very engaging personality. He was very happy and had a real zest for life, he was a complete blessing in our lives," enthused an emotional Mrs Murphy. "Your father would have been very proud of him."

"That's brilliant! I'm happy to hear that. Did he like sport or follow any football team?" asked an expectant Josh.

"He's a massive fan of Manchester United. If you look at his old bedroom, it's still full of Man. Utd memorabilia. He absolutely adores Manchester United. I don't know where he got his love for them, but it's very big," answered Mr Murphy with a smile.

"Oh, that's great," Josh replied, trying desperately to suppress his massive disappointment or even disgust.

"His great hero is Gary Neville. For some reason, he absolutely idolised Gary. You'd think it might have been Ronaldo, Giggs, or Scholes, but no, it's Gary Neville," Mr Murphy went on. "Josh was always chanting that song the fans sing about him."

"Oh yes, I know it," said Josh. And he did. *'Gary Neville is a red, is a red, Gary Neville is a red, he hates Scousers!'*

Josh Stanton was beginning to feel very uncomfortable and annoyed that JJ was, first, a Manchester United fanatic, and second, that his favourite player was one who was feted for allegedly hating Scousers! Josh himself was a very proud Scouser, so he wasn't appreciating what he was hearing at all! He had never liked Manchester United and had even foolishly tried to alter history, such was the contempt he held them in, especially as one their fans had been involved in the fatal car accident involving his dad. Josh knew accidents could happen, but it was the callous way his dad had been left by the United fan that had filled Josh Stanton's often deep hatred of them.

Josh was finding it very hard to mask his displeasure but had to know more about JJ. What was it that Mr and Mrs Murphy had to tell him in person? "Can you tell me how Josh is now? Where is he? I understand he's not with you anymore," he asked keen to get to the nitty-gritty.

Mrs Murphy cleared her throat gently before speaking. "Josh was absolutely wonderful, like we said, but he started changing when reached his teenage years. Something just changed. He became far less joyful, a lot more morose and miserable, and wouldn't talk to us much anymore. He became very insular and withdrawn; it was like a complete and total metamorphosis of the wrong kind. To be honest with you, it's been heart-breaking for us to see such a sprightly, fun person change into the opposite. It was sad to see him leave us, but hopefully he's happier wherever he is."

"That's really disappointing to hear. Is there anything else you can tell me about him that would be useful to know?" Josh sensed there was something bigger to come.

"There are some things that are very unusual about Josh that your father needs to know," explained a sombre Mr Murphy. "First of all, he has displayed very high levels of telepathic ability, and I wouldn't be surprised if he was already well aware of your father and his blood mother and their background. We never told him he was adopted; we were asked explicitly not to divulge anything about his birth by his blood mother. It was her earnest wish for it not to be disclosed, and we decided we could honour that wish if it was for the best. But Josh was aware, and he would bombard us with questions about Marlow and Liverpool. He could display all kinds of perceptive feats." He paused. "How is his mother, by the way?"

That was an extremely painful question for a heartbroken Josh. "I don't know, unfortunately, but I really wish I did. I really miss her," a clearly disconsolate Josh answered.

"Oh, I'm sorry to hear your mum is not around. We can see that you miss her," comforted a sympathetic Mrs Murphy. "There is something else you need to be aware of."

"What's that?" asked a clearly perturbed Josh.

"When he turned thirteen, my husband and I were very concerned about Josh. There was something not right, so we took him for a medical at the doctors. We were very worried and wanted him to be alright, but the doctor discovered something very alarming about him. I think Josh knew there was something very wrong about him, and that's probably why his mood swings changed him for the worst."

"What did the doctors discover?" asked Josh. He was worried that it would be something that he was responsible for, a consequence of JJ being born out of the natural timeline.

Mrs Murphy took a deep breath and, her hand being clasped tightly by her husband, blinked back tears. "The doctors," she said, "found that he was ageing far quicker than he should be. His ageing mechanism was rapid, and his cells were dying off at a far quicker rate than a normal human being. Apparently, this process had only started to kick in, because he was perfectly normal until he was twelve, so happy and then…" Mrs Murphy's voice trailed off as the sadness began to overwhelm her.

Mr Murphy continued where she left off. "The moodiness, petulance, anger was all now there, and we could understand, but we were powerless to help him. We would've done anything for him just to be his former self, but how do you fight physics and biology?"

"How quickly is he ageing?" asked a guilty feeling Josh.

"At first, the rate they were implying was three years to every normal year, but the rate was going to increase as he got older to an estimated ten years to every normal one. So Josh won't get to live a long life unless there's some sort of miracle. We are so incredibly sad, we feel utterly useless for him. I'm not surprised he left," said Mr Murphy, starting to become emotional.

"When did Josh leave you?" Josh questioned.

"It was two years ago, in 2009. He would have been sixteen, but he looked like he was late twenties. It was so incredibly upsetting to see him ageing so quickly and being so helpless to do anything. I think he wanted to be up in the Manchester area as he loved Manchester United, so would very probably want to go somewhere near to his dream place. That's my best guess, as he hasn't been in touch since he left here. You'd think your own son would try and make contact at least once, wouldn't you? I know he's upset, but so are we! We loved him and still do. We would love to know if he's alright, so if you manage to find him, please let us know. You might have more chance of seeing him if he is in your neck of the woods," Mr Murphy implored. "He's your age. You could become friends."

"It's the least I can do," Josh replied, and readied himself to leave. It was obvious Mr and Mrs Murphy had told him everything they could.

At the front door, Mr Murphy paused. "Can I ask you one last thing?"

"Yes, of course," replied Josh.

"Is your dad alright?"

Josh frowned, puzzled. "Yes, why do you ask?"

Mr Murphy shrugged, "Oh, it's just that the doctors were very confused at the physiological make-up of Josh's DNA. It seemed there was a massive difference in his parents' genetic codes, apparently, and I don't for one minute understand but there wa a massive chronological imbalance in the genetic codes. I think this is what has caused Josh's problems."

"Oh, that's unbelievable, but my dad is alright in that sense, thank you." At that, Josh made a hasty exit. He felt terrible, chastising himself for his stupidity and the dreadful consequences it had created. He was already dreading admitting all this to his friend and tutor Mr Xavier Richardson, but he needed any friendly help he could get in this very troubled world and Mr Richardson was most definitely the best person confide in. Josh Stanton deserved everything he would get for his stupidity.

He wasn't expecting to see Mr Xavier Richardson for a couple of weeks, so it could wait. But a massive emotional tsunami was about to break Josh's world as he prepared for bed on returning late home from Cornwall. He was tired, his head full of anguish and guilt, when he heard the phone ring downstairs. *Who could be ringing at 11pm at night?* Josh thought; but relaxed knowing it was likely to be for his mum. She loved to have marathon girlie chats with her friends.

He was just settling down into his bed when he heard her shouting up to him, "Josh, come down, please. You're wanted on the phone urgently."

"Who is it, Mum? What's so urgent? It's 11pm and I'm knackered," he protested. Nevertheless, he complied and headed down to the phone.

"Hello?"

"This is Mrs Chambers, Mrs Anne Chambers, Emma's mother," said a distressed voice at the other end. "Is this Josh Stanton?"

"Yes," he replied.

"I'm sorry to have to tell you that Emma is very poorly in hospital. She's so bad that the doctors have said she might only have a few hours." Mrs Chambers was speaking between sobs. "Emma has asked for you; she wants to see you badly. She asked me to try and get you to come down to see her in hospital. Please come. It could be her dying wish. Come now, if you can, it's urgent. There might not be much time!"

Josh quickly took note of the details then rushed upstairs and dressed quickly. What had happened to Emma? Why was she in hospital? How come, after a year without any contact, he was being contacted and urged to see her in a race against time?

Josh called his friend Mr Xavier Richardson to ask for a gigantic favour, and soon they were powering their way down the M6 and M1 towards London. Josh wished the speed limit was higher, such was the panic-induced anxiety sweeping through him. He hadn't seen Emma for over a year, and this might be the one and only time. How was Emma going to be with him? What would she say to him? Would she even be conscious? Or even worse, would they arrive there too late? Why had Emma suddenly made Josh such a figure of importance?

The only thing for certain was that Josh and Mr Richardson were involved in a mighty dash against the clock. How would it go?

CHAPTER 4

DARKNESS UNDER
A MOONLIGHT SKY

Hurtling down the M1 at a constant 70mph, Josh Stanton was in the passenger seat in a complete and utter daze as London grew closer. Josh was incapable of noticing anything at that moment, all he could think of was his Emma, his poor precious Emma. But Mr Richardson couldn't help noticing the sky as he was driving. It was unusually black, almost pitch black with no heavenly bodies to illuminate its backdrop, no stars twinkling or moon radiating its light, just an unusually black canvas of unremitting darkness. And yet there was no cloud cover; it was crystal clear but no stars were shining. It all seemed a bit weird, but then again Mr Richardson should be tucked up in a nice bed not hammering down the M1 at this time of night, so maybe he was being over dramatic. It did seem odd all the same.

Josh hadn't noticed. His eyes had hardly twitched, his mouth hadn't uttered a word for ages, he was totally in a world of his own, alone and tormented by his thoughts. Mr Richardson could see the grief beginning to manifest itself on Josh's face as he struggled to keep his emotions in check.

"We're nearly there, Josh, won't be long now. I'll drop you off right outside the front entrance, but don't worry I'll park up and meet you inside."

"Thank you, sir. Sorry I've been silent, but I'm scared, I'm so scared. I don't want Emma to die. I love her! I don't know what to do if she dies, my world will feel over completely. I won't want to live! Emma will always be my world, and if she'd not in it I don't want to be in it," replied Josh, completely failing to hide his despair.

"I understand how you feel but you've got to be strong even if it's just for a while. You are there for Emma and for her parents' sake. Try and keep it all in, try and be as strong and positive as you can for them. I know it's not going to be easy but try," urged Mr Richardson. "Remember, the parents are probably bewitched as to your relevance."

"Ok, sir, you're right. I will try very hard for their sakes," responded Josh.

"Good man. Right, we're here now. Someone is waiting for us outside the main entrance."

Josh nodded. "It's Mr Chambers, he's waiting to meet me and take me up to Emma, I'm guessing. Thank you for your help. I owe you everything. I'll see you as soon as I can," said Josh, as he leaned over to hug Mr Richardson.

"Take as long as you need, Josh. Don't forget I remember Emma fondly as well. I'll be waiting in reception for however long you need."

Mr Xavier Richardson was proving to be a great friend to Josh, one of truly massive value. It's a true blessing in life if you're lucky enough to have such a friend who will be there in literally your darkest hour. But now as Josh got out the car, he knew he had to face his immediate destiny and see Emma for the first time in a year. Or it could well be, from Emma's perspective, that it would be for the first time ever, as she had been living a different reality. Josh would have to try to be very brave and keep his emotions in check, but a glimpse at the grief-stricken face of Mr Chambers left him in no doubt as to the severity of the situation.

"Thank you so much for coming down at such short notice, but we couldn't wait to contact you. I have to warn you that Emma is very poorly," Mr Chambers said. "She... she hasn't got long to live. She had a very bad fall, but she won't tell us how. We have our suspicions, but she wants us to forget about all the whys and wherefores. That is her fervent wish, so I guess that's what we will have to do, but how can we?"

As they approached intensive care, Josh was warned to take a massive breath before going in. It was going to be very traumatic for him to see Emma lying virtually lifeless, with her time running low. In the time that was left, every second would be of paramount importance and grasped with massive gratitude. Emma was barely conscious, her grip on life extremely tenuous. But she was awake, which was at least something to be extremely grateful for.

Josh focused his eyes intently on Emma for the first time in a year. Yes, she was distressingly fragile and poorly, but she was still beautiful. Absolutely beautiful! How Josh had missed seeing her, and now here she was but had so little time! Her eyes registered a knowing acceptance that Josh was present, and she managed a smile as she offered her right hand for him to hold.

Josh could no longer hide his emotions as he held her hand and poured out his heart. He never wanted to let go of her hand. Fighting his severe trauma, he was extremely grateful to at least be able to share her final moments and to see her beautiful smile. He held up his left hand, the ring obvious on his middle finger.

"You see that ring?" he whispered. "It's from you. It's our friendship ring, which you gave me on my seventeenth birthday." Josh felt Emma's hand tighten round his and could see that she was trying hard to muster up enough energy to talk.

"It's alright, Emma, I'm with you. You're very special, you've always been incredibly special! I love you so much."

Josh was trying so hard not to burst into tears and leaned forward as Emma showed an almost superhuman show of determination to whisper, "I remember you. I love you, too."

With that, Josh could feel Emma's grip loosen as the final tiny breath was taken, and Emma's life force had finally gone.

"NO! NO! NO! Please, NO!" Josh and Mr and Mrs Chambers called out in anguish.

All three were utterly inconsolable with grief. It was 3am in the morning and this was the most horrendous night of Josh Stanton's life. The unbearable darkness in Josh's heart was darker than a night under a moonless sky with no stars. The lack of stars shining tonight was as though heaven knew something; it was like heaven was mourning as well.

Josh didn't want to leave the intensive care room. He never wanted to leave Emma, but she had taken her last breath and was now completely devoid of life. Before he left, he gazed for some time at her beautiful face, and could no longer control the tidal wave of tears that were streaming down his cheeks. He felt like a broken man! He still did not know how Emma had managed to recognise him, or why it had taken so long, but this wasn't the time to ask questions. it was time to mourn, and it would take him an eternity to even begin recovering from this. Josh didn't even know if he wanted to recover at all!

Josh met Mr Richardson and prepared for the tortuous journey home. At least his friend could understand to a degree what Josh must be thinking. He was more determined than ever to try to find a miracle, a miracle that was needed to get back to the past and reset and untangle the natural timeline. It was never supposed to be like this! The emotional pain Josh was feeling was so intense, but he had to use all his energies to somehow find a way to return to the past. He needed divine help from somewhere.

As Josh and Mr Richardson left the M6, it was now nearly 6am. It had been a horrendously painful night, but in a sense a wondrous one as well, because Josh had actually seen Emma for one last time. It was a tiny consolation. His tears had given way to a morbid silence during the trip home; not a word was uttered for hours, there was just a very solemn silence, Mr Richardson could understand all this, but as he approached Liverpool and Josh's home, he wanted to utter some comfort to his badly shaken young friend.

"We're nearly at your house now," he said. "I know you don't want to talk, but I'm going to try my best to work something out. If it has to take me years, I'm going to do my best for... for Emma..."

"Thank you, sir. I know you will. You're a fantastic person, sir. I will repay all your kindness at some point, because I owe you so much," said a very sad but grateful Josh. There was a moment or two of silence, then Josh asked, "Sir, have you ever been in true love? Have you ever had anybody truly special in your life?"

Josh had grown a deep bond and friendship with Mr Richardson but didn't really know too much about the man's personal life. He was curious to know more about this man who was becoming a better friend by the day, as well as being an extremely clever person who offered a glimmer of hope in Josh's devastated world. But Mr Richardson's answer saddened Josh.

"Goodness, no! I've never been lucky enough to meet someone special and experience true love. I think I never will, as I can't see anybody loving me for who I am. I'm too geeky and unorthodox for anybody to understand. I think that's why I devote a lot of energy into my science background. I've channelled my focus away from trying not to dream about finding true love, as I think for me it would be extremely elusive to find; it would be a case of wasted mental energy."

"That's truly sad, sir. You're a very kind, clever, and good person, and you've helped me in my darkest hour when I needed you and proved to be a true friend. That is very valuable, sir. I think you deserve to meet someone special, and they do say there is someone out there for everyone," Josh replied sympathetically.

"Not for me, there isn't," protested a disbelieving Mr Richardson. "I've come to accept this; I've come to accept I won't find true love."

"I don't believe you, sir! You can supply brilliant theories on time travel and explain all the amazing intricacies they present, but you're telling me that you are unable to believe you can find love? I don't believe you, sir! And I don't believe you don't care either, as everybody wants and needs to be loved. Please let me tell you this. If you're lucky enough to find true love, it's the most wonderful, glorious feeling in the world. It's incredibly powerful and can totally dominate your mind, completely obliterating everything else into a pitiful mundaneness. Nothing else seems to matter, that person is the total centre of your whole universe. You can feel your heart literally race, sense it pumping furiously. You can feel butterflies floating throughout your body as you anticipate seeing her, your heart literally aches with yearning. True love can conquer everything! To experience true love from a woman that you love is the greatest force anyone can ever know! That's what I had with Emma Chambers." Josh paused briefly. "I hope you can experience what I experienced. I truly hope I can experience it again. If I ever get over Emma or if I never can see her again, I hope I will eventually see someone as uniquely special. I know I would be incredibly lucky. I know that for a fact."

Josh could have talked literally for hours on the subject, but they had now arrived back at his home in Gwladys Street, Liverpool.

Before he got out of the car, he added, "I have to say, though, that once true love gets hold of you it is like it will never let go, no matter how hard you try. It has an absolute vice-like grip on your heart and can leave you a total prisoner to it. True love is absolutely amazing, but it can be very harmful to your emotional wellbeing as well. The hurt you feel is intensified massively to an intolerance level should there be something that goes wrong. True love does make you very vulnerable."

"Wow, you are an expert on the meaning of love! You've certainly given me a lesson," Mr Richardson replied with a smile.

"Let me give you an analogy, sir," Josh offered.

"Go on then. I love analogies!"

"I know you do, sir!" Josh replied. "Imagine true love is like a tube of superglue. What would happen if you smeared it on my fingers?"

"They'd completely stick together and would be very hard, if not impossible, to pull apart once the bond has stuck," Mr Richardson answered.

"Yes exactly, that's what it is with true love," said Josh. "Once the bond is stuck between the fingers, it represents two people and it is very hard if not impossible to pull them apart.

"I see what you are trying to tell me, Josh. Thank you for that. I can see that true love is special and that you've been very lucky. Perhaps there might be someone for me somewhere, but please excuse my sceptical view that there probably won't be. I do appreciate your enthusiasm, though," remarked a candid Mr Richardson.

As Josh left Mr Richardson's car, he realised he had momentarily enjoyed a brief respite from his inner torment and found a little solace from his conversation with his friend. It had been therapeutic to talk about another person's standpoint and ascertain how they felt about things, particularly when reality was persistently painful to be in.

Josh felt intense gloom return as he entered his bedroom. His mood was as intense and dark as the moonless sky, with no stars shining their welcoming twinkling of light. There seemed no illumination or chink of light to be found in Josh's heart. It was going to take a long time, a very long time, for the divine miracle. Where, when, and how would it come?

Footnote

When the visitor from the end of the world imitates (from his smart-watch) a time bubble, it is from an apocalyptic future 2045. Preceding his arrival in Liverpool in 2011, there was a massive electrical storm, caused by static from the bubble being induced under such apocalyptic conditions in which it originated, and now had manifested itself in the shape of a phenomenal electrical storm ahead of the visitor's arrival. In essence, this was time static.

CHAPTER 5

THE VISITOR FROM
THE END OF THE WORLD

DECEMBER 24TH, 2011

The end of another year was fast approaching, and Christmas had arrived almost unnoticed. It had been a horrible year to endure for Josh, the ultimate *annus horribilis;* 2011 would forever hold traumatically terrible memories for him. For the second year running, Josh didn't feel like celebrating Christmas. There was no goodwill in his spirit, there had been no sign of a miracle anywhere, and no matter how hard Josh tried, he was no nearer moving on. Liverpool FC were showing signs of a promising season under King Kenny, but poor Josh couldn't summon up enough happiness to embrace this. He was the epitome of misery!

There was only one thing Josh wanted for Christmas and that was for Emma to be alive again and in his life, but it all seemed a totally forlorn hope. Christmas Eve was proving truly torturous, as there was happiness and celebrations happening all around him, and Josh was finding it unbearable! The weather was ice cold and uninviting, and snow had flirted intermittently during the day. There was no way Josh was going to the local club. He was going to bed with extra sleeping tablets to make sure he didn't wake up until Boxing Day!

It was only 7pm when Josh went upstairs to his bedroom; his sleep was likely to be very deep and very long. Wrong! As midnight approached, Josh had indeed been in deep sleep, but by now he was aware of the very loud weather outside. He could hear a strong, howling, whistling wind making an almighty din as it threatened to cause havoc, and Josh could actually feel the house shake. It was pretty scary!

Josh got out of bed and looked out of the window as the sound of massive thunderclaps boomed out, penetrating his very soul and giving him a massive jolt!

"This is very strange," Josh muttered to himself. "There was no mention of any thunderstorms in the weather forecast. It was supposed to be ice cold and very calm, with little or no wind, maybe even a little snow on Christmas Day it was suggested. Yet now there is an almighty thunderstorm brewing outside, how can this be?"

He continued to look out of the window. *Thunderstorms are normally a product of hot air, not cold air. This is very strange!* Josh thought. *It looks unreal!*

Josh felt very unsettled and was mesmerised by the very angry sky enveloping Stanley Park, forked lightning now providing a foreboding kaleidoscope of danger amongst its purple backdrop. The sky was raging! Its energy was frighteningly fierce as the lightning appeared to strike simultaneously in several places in a very impressive, but scary, visual display of intricate symmetry. It was a truly wondrous panorama!

He stood transfixed for at least an hour, as the storm and its heavy yield of rain passed over. Josh looked at his radio clock, which said 1.45. He was beginning to feel drowsy again, so climbed back into bed. Was this all a silly dream? It didn't make sense, but this was a portent to an arrival that would be immensely important to Josh. This crazy weather phenomenon had been an artificial precursor to the arrival of a very special person.

The radio clock was showing the time as 3.30, and Josh was in a deep sleep when again there was a sense of growing electrical activity. This time, it was much closer. It was coming from within Josh's own bedroom! He woke with a startlingly swift jolt and opened his eyes; he couldn't believe what he was seeing.

It was a time bubble, but much smaller in diameter, probably about 7ft in height and maybe only 3ft wide, and there was what looked like a 25-year-old man sitting inside this bubble! The man had a strange-looking device on his left arm, like an ultra-special smartphone which was flashing green.

Josh was rigid with shock. He didn't know what to think as his brain struggled to explain its rationale of seeing this time bubble with a man inside. Suddenly the bubble began dissipating around the man, leaving him exposed to fully engage with a terrified Josh.

But thankfully, this visitor couldn't have been friendlier as he greeted an absolutely stunned Liverpudlian.

"Don't be alarmed. I'm here to help you save the world. This is the greatest day of my life! I can't believe I'm actually seeing you AGAIN," said the visitor.

"Again? Again? What do you mean again? I've never seen you before!" a truly amazed Josh protested.

"I know what you must be thinking. You must be extremely confused but you have met me, it's just you haven't met me YET!" replied the visitor. "You must have thousands of questions as to what is going on: Who am I? What's my name? How am I going to help you? You already know I'm here to help you save the world, but I bet you've got thousands of questions, haven't you?"

"You're not kidding!!" Josh answered.

"Go on then, fire away," the visitor said with enthusiasm.

"Ok, what's your name?" asked Josh.

"My name is Stevie, Stevie Jamie Xabi Luis... STANTON! I was named in honour of Steven Gerrard."

"STANTON!" Josh repeated, shocked. "Are you related to me?"

"I'd say so. You are my dad! I'm from the future," explained the visitor. "I was born on June 14th, 2020, and I've now come back to see you from the year 2045! But I have to tell you it's not entirely unselfish act, because the world is falling apart and collapsing under the strain of realities colliding. The piece of time elastic is snapping, so in a way I've escaped to see you, but my existence in any future is unclear and this journey I've undertaken is a one-way journey. My journey ends here. My aim is to help you, and it can only be you to restore the timeline to the way it was supposed to be before time and different realities got tangled up." Josh stared in astonishment as this visitor who'd now revealed himself to be Stevie, Josh's possible future son!

"Wow!" he breathed, when he finally found his voice again. "How have you managed to find a time bubble? How can you manipulate it so easily? How come it's much smaller than what I expected?"

"Let me explain everything for you," said the visitor calmly. "First things first. I have the same blood type as you, being your son. I'm very fortunate that I do as, for some unknown reason, only people with AB Negative blood can manage to penetrate and withstand a time bubble and it can only be done once or twice before it gets too intense. It's not something you can keep using, it's definitely finite!

"Now, it's true the bubble is smaller than what you would have been thinking of. To give you a comparison, think of computers in your father's time, they were massive, weren't they? They could fill half a room, but as years advanced they were reduced to an unbelievably small size, yet they were just as powerful.

Technology in 2045 is incredibly advanced, and after years and years of painstaking research it has become possible to induce a time bubble and control its settings. We were all becoming extremely aware there was something extremely wrong with the world, so the urge to try and do something was enormous. And as I am able to withstand and penetrate a time bubble, I was the perfect choice – and especially as this is personal, very personal. I can't believe I am seeing you my own dad again. I'm so happy! You were an absolutely fantastic dad, you really were."

Stevie was becoming quite emotional, and although Josh was very touched, he still wanted to know lots more.

"Thank you for saying all those nice things, but how can you control these time bubbles?" he asked.

"Oh, that was the work of my project partner. She had a brilliant mind that could operate on a different level to anybody else. She was like a gift from God in the way she could work out all the many different correlations and intricacies of time, and she managed to devise this brilliant smart-watch that you can see on my left arm. It's a Chronologically Temporal Sensitive Super Smart Time watch, or a C.T.S.S.S.T for short. It's an absolutely brilliant piece of work, quite probably the greatest creation ever. Gabriella was a brilliant woman." The visitor paused and smiled. "I was in awe of her. I don't know how she managed to be so brilliant, but it seemed like she was working under divine inspiration. Do you want to look at this smart-watch?"

"Yes, please," a keen Josh answered.

"Alright, but you must absolutely not touch anything! It's all pre-set, and you risk ruining your one chance to return to the past if you press or touch anything you shouldn't."

"Ok, I understand," replied Josh. Then the penny dropped! Josh suddenly realised he was going to be using the smart-watch to return to the past, to undo all the wrongs he'd initiated, to untie the knot he had helped create. Stevie had come back to give him this gift of hope! Tears began to swell in Josh's eyes as the full implications of Stevie's visit hit home.

"Please don't cry," urged Stevie. "This is the greatest day of my life now, that I can see you again."

"Again? You keep saying again. Wasn't I alive in 2045? I would only be 52 myself in 2045, so why do you keep saying again?" Josh was puzzled. His tears were giving way to anxiety.

"You disappeared, Dad! You just disappeared in the year 2030 and were never seen again. I was only ten years old at the time and I was absolutely devastated, because you were a brilliant dad and did everything with me. I cried and cried my eyes out. So did my mum. It was a complete mystery that not even Gabriella could explain to me or even offer a plausible explanation or theory," a clearly emotional Stevie answered.

"Oh my goodness, how strange! I don't know why I would disappear or even want to disappear, especially when it sounds like I was extremely happy being your dad!" remarked Josh. Then another question suddenly occurred to him. "Your mum? Who is she? Have I met her yet?" His heart raced as he waited for Stevie's answer.

"My mother is called Donna. Donna Taylor. You haven't met her yet, but you will in the next two or three years, if Gabriella's calculations are correct. She's got beautiful blonde hair, and lots of people told me she was stunning to look at. I think you will be very pleasantly surprised! Donna is still alive in 2045, and I love her and want her to live and not suffer the collapse of time. She was with me as I entered the time bubble and she was inconsolable as I disappeared from her view." Stevie paused briefly. "That is another reason why this visit is so important. I need my mum to be saved. I want humanity to be saved. No pressure then!" He smiled, trying to strike a lighter note.

Josh's heart felt a little lighter for the first time in what seemed years. He examined Stevie's mighty impressive smart-watch and couldn't help noticing the face of the watch had a set time showing: 7pm/19.00 hours; 1st October 1990; location... Marlow! The Ploughman's Inn, Marlow!

"What's this?" Josh asked.

"It's the pre-set time, date, and location that you will be sent to when the time is ready to send you back. You will be wearing this watch to enable you to engage a time bubble and make sure it sends you to the optimum time and place to re-mend the natural timeline," Stevie answered.

"What do I have to do while I'm there? Do you know exactly what I have to do?" Josh asked.

"Yes. This is by far the most important question you have asked me, and I'm really sorry but you're going to hate my answer!" Stevie warned.

"Why will I hate it?"

"Your lifesaving mission to re-set time to its natural course is that you have to stop Emma Chambers from falling in love with you."

Stevie's answer was absolutely devastating for Josh! Surely there was a mistake in the calculations. Emma was a magical piece of Josh's heart and soul. Surely there had to be another way?

"Are you sure? Are you totally sure?" Josh protested.

"I'm really sorry but it is of paramount importance. I'll explain for you. Emma Chambers was always destined to meet and marry a Michael Smith, who just happened to be in the pub on the night you're going back to. Apparently he was on the verge of breaking up an engagement to go back to Emma, who was his childhood sweetheart, but by now Emma was falling in love with this stranger from the north who was joining in the pub quizzes with her parents... who, of course, was you! This stopped Michael and Emma getting together, as Emma loved you more. So they never went on to have their baby daughter in 1995. They were supposed to have a daughter called Katie, who was destined to be an extremely important person in the world, as a future peace envoy. She was an extremely pivotal figure in the balance of peace within our borders, but thanks to your unintended meddling there was now no Katie Chambers-Smith! This was a crucial loss which you helped to create unfortunately, and it absolutely has to be corrected," Stevie explained.

"Why is October 1st the D-day?" Josh asked.

"October 1st was the point of no return, as by then all Emma needed from you was confirmation that you felt the same as her, to seal true love. You supplied that by asking her out and making your feelings known to her. It was all she needed to know, as apparently there was an intense chemistry between you already, something that was very hard to ignore. I'm really sorry, but you have to shatter her dreams of being in love with you and it being reciprocated. It's going to be very painful, as I suspect you loved her very much, but I know if you truly loved Emma you'd want her to be happy, with a wonderful daughter." Stevie looked closely to Josh. "I understand she's not alive today, is she?"

"No, she isn't," Josh replied sadly. "Emma died as I held her hand half a year ago. I don't want her to not live her natural life, I love her too much. I couldn't bear seeing her die! I want her to be happy, and if that was supposed to be with Michael, then I know what I have to do. I'm ready to go back to the past."

"That's great, but it's not the right moment yet," Stevie said.

"Why's that? You've told me what needs to be done and I am ready to do it," Josh was anxious for his infernal nightmare to end for good.

"I'm afraid you have to be in the right place in the right moment to be able to activate this smart-watch. It is already pre-set for a time and place before it can be activated; it has all been pre-calculated from a predestined location at a predestined time, so it won't be accurate unless it's done at that precise time, date and location. When the time is right, the watch will illuminate green, ready for you to execute and initiate the time bubble which will send you back to its pre-set time, date, and location, which you already know as Marlow 1990."

"Ok, but what is the predestined time, date and location that I can proceed to initiate the time bubble then?"

Stevie proceeded to show his smart-watch again to Josh and pressed the forwarding display button. There was Josh's predestined time, date and location for forward travel to the past: May 13th, 2012, 6pm; Ashton Canal, outside Manchester City's Etihad Stadium.

"Etihad Stadium? Manchester City's ground? Why am I going to be there when I am a big fan of Liverpool? Is that date a Saturday?" Josh asked.

Josh proceeded to look at his football calendar and it wasn't a Saturday, but it was a Sunday. It was the last Sunday of the Premier League Season! How could Josh even think of being at Manchester City's Etihad Stadium when it was obvious that he would want to be supporting Liverpool at their last game of the season, which was Swansea City away – a place many miles from Manchester. Josh was going to be stunned by Stevie's answer.

"Something is going to happen during this match that will totally alter the course of football history and it is a person you won't recognise but you will feel terribly responsible for. All I'm telling you is that it involves your unnatural son that you and Emma made when you were in the throes of blissful love, a love that should never have happened!" Stevie told him. "I can also tell you that this match was supposed to be the greatest dramatic match in the history of the Premier League. Anyone present at the Etihad Stadium on May 13th, 2012 will never forget the day they were there, or the many millions of people watching on television. You will, or should, be very privileged to be there, or at least that's the way it should've been until your son shows up and spoils it. Be very shocked at what you see! But once the game is over and you initiate the bubble at a discreet place next to the Ashton Canal, outside and near the Stadium, and execute your mission successfully, the smart-watch will automatically return you to the Etihad Stadium for 4pm on May 13th, 2012, so you can see the natural timeline restored. The smart-watch will no longer be on your arm when you re-appear, if everything in the natural timeline has been correctly re-set. So you will know if you were successful, and you will get to see the greatest finish to a Premier League season you will ever see. Please take my advice... whatever you do, don't leave early!"

This was totally awesome, mind-blowing information that Josh was being bombarded with, not least that he would have sight of JJ (Josh junior) for possibly the first time, but that it was going to be bad. Did it have to be this way? Stevie had explained that this part of history had to be played out, and every calculation made with regards his smart-watch was made taking this match into account. It had to be remembered that JJ had been born completely outside the normal rules of time and was going to directly influence a part of the timeline affecting millions of people, but he had to be allowed to complete his life in the course it was taking and then disappear. This was the 'Temporal Bleeding' that had been mentioned by Mr Xavier Richardson in conversation with Josh about time being a 'radiator'. So, JJ was like an air pocket within the system, and when JJ disappeared so would the air pocket, meaning when Josh tries to repair the timeline in the past there is no longer an air pocket in the system to jeopardise the repair!

Stevie had said JJ would just fade out of existence on the day he ruins the greatest match, sometime around 5pm on that day, whilst in the company of Greater Manchester Police. It couldn't be explained, but JJ did totally live out of the normal rules of time so normal rules didn't apply to him, and it was for the world to be eternally grateful.

Josh Stanton knew in theory that he faded from existence when he was conceived by his parents – at least, his version that wasn't supposed to be there. Maybe this was a parallel situation; JJ was not supposed to be there; he was never supposed be there! But maybe time had found its own way or, as in the case of many air pockets, they can be present and then they're gone!

Josh Stanton looked at his radio clock. It was now showing 6am and he was really tired. He needed his sleep even though it was Christmas morning. Stevie sensed the growing fatigue of his dad and stated his intention to leave.

"Where will you go? You won't be activating your smart-watch, so where will you go?" asked Josh.

"Don't worry, Josh – I mean, Dad – everything is ok and sorted. I've got a place to stay nearby so you will see lots of me during the next few months. I've been dreaming of seeing you again. This is a really precious time for me, and a very special one as you are my dad. I'm going to experience the Premier League with you, and watch Liverpool with you. The Premier League no longer exists in my time – you don't know how special it is. You shouldn't take it for granted," Stevie said as he peered out of Josh Stanton's front window. "Wow! Goodison Park! Everton FC! I can't believe I'm seeing a truly historical football ground," he said. "I can't wait to go Anfield with you and see all the other fantastic grounds and experience watching it on TV. You don't realise how lucky you are!"

It was good to see Stevie awestruck for once! How would he be seeing his actual namesake, Stevie G, playing for the mighty Reds? He was going to be amazed! Josh could go to sleep much happier than he'd been a few hours earlier, but still with the knowledge that he had a heart-breaking mission to perform in the future. However, it was for the better good and there was clear light at the end of the tunnel, and in the meantime Josh had met a very exciting visitor – a visitor from the end of the world!

Josh was about to say farewell to his special new-found friend – indeed, his future son – and then it dawned on him that his friend Mr Xavier Richardson would absolutely love to meet this visitor from the future. Mr Xavier Richardson would find Stevie fascinating in the extreme.

"I want you to meet my good friend, Mr Xavier Richardson," Josh said. But he didn't expect Stevie's reply.

"I know Xavier Richardson very well indeed. It will be fantastic to see him again, especially as a middle-aged man. I only know him as an elderly gentleman."

Josh was stunned. "You've met Xavier? You know him? How do you know him?" he asked.

"Mr Xavier Richardson is the father of Gabriella, my project partner and owner of a brilliant mind," Stevie explained. "She's Gabriella Richardson, the daughter of Xavier Richardson and Isabella Rossi. She was born in 2022, so she's just a bit younger than me but a lot cleverer. She inherited a lot of good brainpower from her parents."

With that absolute bombshell, Stevie departed. How was Josh supposed to sleep after being told that? He couldn't wait to see Mr Xavier Richardson and tell him what he'd learnt from Stevie; he especially couldn't wait to inform Xavier that he was going to be in a relationship, marry, and have a wonderfully gifted daughter! Josh would pay good money to see the look on his friend's face when he told him. It was going to absolutely priceless!

Josh remembered all Xavier's protestations about being uniquely unlovable and how he would never encounter love, so the prospect of Mr Xavier Richardson being in a steady relationship was extremely intriguing; absolute gold! Josh would give everything to be present when Mr Xavier Richardson met Isabella Rossi for the first time! To judge his reaction would be golden.

Mr Xavier Richardson was away during the festive break, so it would have to wait until next month when Josh was back at college to meet up. Josh couldn't wait to see him, but then a tiny bit of apprehensive doubt crept into Josh's mind... Was this the way it was supposed to be? Was Mr Xavier Richardson always going to find love and have a daughter? Or was all this a product of tangled timelines, and realities? When Josh eventually went back in time and unravelled all the knots that helped him create and restore the (straight) natural timeline, who in the future would still be real? Through all sorts of liaisons, there would be people together by now who were never supposed to meet, indeed people alive that were never due to be born. And, conversely, there were people that were supposed to be alive that were never born now, and Josh knew that one of those was a Katie Chambers-Smith.

Josh was struck with chilled wonder! Was he always destined to meet Donna Taylor and have a fantastic son, Stevie? Or again, was it a product of tangled realities? There was more mystery than the depth of the Grand Canyon! But there was no use worrying about it; he would just have to see where time would naturally take things and go with the natural flow. If it was meant to be, it was meant to be!

As Josh settled back down into a deep sleep, he couldn't suppress a huge grin on his face. Mr Xavier Richardson, you sly old fox!

CHAPTER 6

PRECIOUS

It was the first day of term at Manchester College, and Josh had anticipated this day with such great relish. He couldn't wait to see Mr Richardson and disclose everything, and maybe give him a little gentle but respectful teasing. There had been a massive potential breakthrough with Stevie's visit, so hope had soared along with Josh's spirits.

During the last week or so, Josh had regularly seen Stevie and there was a great bond developing between them. Josh only ever saw his son on his own, as Stevie was always stressing how it was still very important even in this fragmented and fractured time that Stevie didn't do anything or meet anybody that would even slightly alter the time dynamics. Every calculation of time had been meticulously balanced for Stevie's smart-watch to operate at the optimum efficiency, and it could be seriously compromised with any undue unforeseen incident. But there was room, or enough margins, for Stevie to be able to spend time with Josh. And that included football matches, as long as Stevie didn't directly engage with anybody else. Stevie could only directly involve himself with Josh, so unfortunately Josh wouldn't be able to introduce Stevie directly even to Mr Xavier Richardson, and he would have to be careful even in what he told his friend, such were the subtle vagaries of time sensitivity. Everything Josh wanted to say to Mr Richardson would have to be cleared first with Stevie.

Stevie did have a great guide to the effectiveness of his mission, however. If there was imminent danger of temporal shift, his smart-watch would flash red and he would have to rectify and address any issues. This was extremely useful in his mission, but there was room for Stevie to enjoy this precious time with Josh so long as he was very careful. Spending time with his dad, even for only a few months, was something Stevie cherished like a precious jewel.

Stevie had the capacity to experience a preselected few football matches with Josh, handpicked with extreme caution and with all part of the calculations made. His ultimate dream while existing in 2012 was to experience the Premier League sensations. Stevie knew he was witnessing history, a truly golden era of football, and a chance to watch the mighty Liverpool with his namesake playing for them: the legendary Stevie Gerrard! To be able to watch it all with his beloved father was heavenly! Pure utopia! Especially as it included a League Cup final at Wembley Stadium in March.

Stevie was going to Wembley with Josh in March to see Liverpool being successful – without being warned in advance; enjoyment is best experienced spontaneously. This period of time was going to be fantastic for them both, and extremely precious!

Back at Manchester College, Josh was able to see Mr Xavier Richardson at long last.

"Hello, sir, have you had a nice break?" he asked.

"Yes, I did, thank you. What about you, Josh, are you any happier? I know you were dreading Christmas, weren't you?" Mr Richardson replied.

"I was, and I did. I was an absolute misery guts! But then something happened on Christmas Eve, sir, that has completely turned around my mood," Josh said with total honesty.

"What was it?" Mr Richardson asked. "It must have been something incredible to change your mood!"

"It was. I had a visitor," Josh replied, his mischievous grin betraying an urge to play with his friend before giving him the awe-inspiring news that Mr Richardson was going to find love.

"Must have been a special visitor, they've cheered you right up! Did they come a long way?" Mr Richardson asked.

"Oh, I'd say so! He came from the end of the world, and just so happens to be my future son, so I'd say he was a little bit special!" answered Josh, and then stood waiting for Mr Richardson's response.

"My goodness, that is one special visitor!" Mr Richardson looked stunned. "I am presuming and hoping you're going to tell me that a time bubble is involved and that we now have hope?"

"Absolutely. We have also got something that can actually control the contortions of time travel. It's a fantastic smart-watch – a CTSSS, for short – it's a chronological, temporal sensitive, super smart, time watch. I will be going back to the past but not just yet. I can tell you it will be in May this year," Josh explained. "Would you like to know more about the woman who created this super smart-watch, sir? She's a genius, after all!"

"Of course. She sounds fantastic; a saviour of the world no less, if you can work your magic in the past. What's her name?" asked Mr Richardson.

"Oh, it's Gabriella," Josh answered, and then he could hold his excitement back no more as he continued, "Gabriella Richardson! Daughter of a Mr Xavier Richardson and, apparently, an Isabella Rossi…"

Xavier Richardson, totally and utterly dumbstruck, was unable to utter a single word for what seemed ages. And even then, he seemed to be struggling to accept the magnitude of what Josh had just told him.

"Impossible! Impossible!" he protested. "You must be misinformed or mistaken! There's no way I can see any possibility, any possibility at all, that I will be involved in any romantic hanky-panky, let alone produce a brilliant daughter. It's impossible! I've long come to accept love isn't for me; it's not going to happen! No way. And anyway, I'm not into anything Italian which I'm guessing she sounds like. The only thing I like Italian is spaghetti Bolognese! I'm sorry, but you've been misled."

"Sir, you protest too much," laughed Josh. "Just relax. You're going to find love whether you like it or not. Don't fight it, you'll enjoy it!"

Josh wasn't managing to convince Mr Richardson at this moment in time but was revelling mischievously in his friend's discomfort in a gentle sort of way. Mr Richardson deserved to find love and happiness, even if he didn't want to find it. Josh also informed Mr Richardson that Stevie had advised him that he had to be very careful what could be divulged in case it made time fluctuate off its calculated pre-set pattern.

Knowing how intricate time was, Mr Richardson appreciated the delicacy of the situation, but reminded Josh that he was always there should he need his advice.

With everything now set up and in place for Josh's revisit to the past, the stresses and strains of this vital mission could be put on hold until May, leaving him time to enjoy Stevie's company while he could. Josh knew better than most that life was too short not to. He was determined to seize the day and the moment, knowing that an unforeseen circumstance could completely rock his world and leave it spinning uncontrollably on its axis! *Now I know you have to treasure every day, to treasure life and your time living it as a very precious gift*, he thought.

Stevie had already made it plain that he was starry-eyed at being around the golden age of the Premier League and having the chance to see the fantastic football grounds around the country. He was also incredibly excited at the prospect of seeing his lifetime hero and namesake, Steven Gerrard, playing in the flesh! Josh couldn't wait to witness the unbridled joy it would bring to Stevie to see Steven Gerrard play for Liverpool! He would be like a five-year-old boy on Christmas Eve, awaiting the arrival of Santa.

For Josh, this time was going to be truly precious! It was going to be lads' time – a time for Josh and Stevie to enjoy the moment and embrace it. Stevie had already intimated to Josh that Liverpool would have some great moments during the second half of the season and, without giving anything away, there might, just might, be a trophy to be won! Stevie knew what was coming, but it wasn't going to stop him enjoying every second. And a lot of the fun would be experiencing it with his beloved dad and seeing the joy on Josh's face when Liverpool won! It was going to be very precious to see!!

JANUARY 2012-MAY 11TH, 2012 (2 days before Man. City v QPR)

(Football Heaven!)

11th January 2012 saw Liverpool away to Manchester City in the League Cup Semi-Final 1st leg at the Etihad Stadium. This was an absolute must-see in Josh's adopted city of Manchester, and the scene of the tumultuous, forthcoming, final day of the season. Man. City were flying and quite probably the best team in the country. They were champions-in-waiting, so for Liverpool to face Man. City was the hardest possible draw. But Wembley was the tantalising reward for the winners over two legs, and Josh would've 'bitten your hand off' if he'd been told Liverpool could have a draw in this first leg or even accept a narrow defeat, such was the greatness of Man. City.

Josh and Stevie arrived early at the Etihad to survey the area nearby at Ashton Canal, where Josh was going to be when he activated the smart-watch and be sure of every logistic. Stevie loved the sight of the Etihad, Man. City's very impressive former Commonwealth stadium. Approaching the ground, it gave off the unique aura of a giant spider, such was the unique design with the position of its supporting pillars. As Josh and Stevie watched the match from the away south stand, Josh couldn't help noticing the picture board situated in the far corner showing the blue moon, which was Man. City's signature feature; it was a captivating sight to behold.

Josh and Stevie were loving being amongst the passionate hordes of Liverpool fans completely filling both tiers of the south stand; at least 7,000 away Liverpool fans were creating a carnival atmosphere. The match was going like a dream as Liverpool soaked up lots of Man. City pressure, then scored a goal themselves. The Liverpool fans went wild and almost knocked Josh and Stevie completely off their feet!

Josh was ecstatic, but Stevie was as white as a sheet. "What's wrong? This is brilliant! We're in dreamland!" Josh said.

"I know but we've just avoided a terrible disaster! All that pushing and shoving nearly knocked my smart-watch completely off," replied Stevie, looking shaken. "Next time we need to be much more careful not to be right amongst the madness when we score. Whenever I know something's going to happen, we'll keep our way out of the madness. We can't afford for anything to go wrong! I'm not used to such raw passion; it is totally different in the future."

"What do you mean?" asked Josh. "Are you saying the passion has died in the future? I can't imagine Liverpool fans just politely applauding like a theatre audience. Liverpool fans are the greatest, they exude raw passion, and I can't ever see that changing." Josh looked sceptical but Stevie's reply left him rocked to his very core!

"Dad, there is no Liverpool FC after 2029!"

"What! You can't be serious! No Liverpool? Liverpool would never be allowed to die; they are a massive worldwide institution! There is no way I believe that!" Josh was incandescent with rage at the suggestion.

"Liverpool don't totally disappear or die. They just amalgamate and join forces with another club, to be accepted into the North Atlantic Super League. It was compulsory. They had no choice," explained Stevie. "The Premier League was blown away by the staggering rise of USA football and the desire to join their football and marry it with the cream of European leagues. The USA acquired all the power and could call the shots. They wanted the European teams to merge into their neighbours, as the demand for places within the N.A.S.L were enormous. You had no choice if you wanted to join it, and Liverpool were extremely reluctant, but it was the best of two very bad options as football in the UK was dying due to total greed and apathy. The only exception in the UK that could stay the same and not amalgamate was Manchester United, and they have to call themselves The Manchester Red Devils. They saw Manchester City completely disintegrate as a consequence of the devastating result on the last day of this season, something that was massively influenced to deviate from what it should be by your son born out of natural time. The Man. City v QPR match was the day football was put on a very treacherous alternative path – you'd hate it! Absolutely hate it!" Stevie added.

"I detest the sound of it already," Josh said. "Who do Liverpool join forces with? Do I need to guess?"

Stevie nodded. "Everton Football Club, that's right. Goodison Park and Anfield were bulldozed in 2029, and a super stadium was built in Stanley Park by 2030. The trouble was that by now money was extremely tight, and the conditions in the world had deteriorated to such an extent that football, even in Liverpool, was becoming less and less important. Both Liverpool and Everton fans absolutely hated the new set-up and completely shunned the new stadium. It was like a massive white elephant, and completely soulless. And people hated being bossed around by those upstarts from the USA."

Stevie paused briefly before continuing. "The Premier League was magnificent in its time. Please believe me when I say you don't know what you've got until it's gone. This is why I am so excited to experience these games with you while I can; it is so, so precious."

"I believe you," Josh replied, his memory focusing on his last painful day with Emma Chambers. "By the way, what do Liverpool and Everton call themselves? How did they get around their name?"

"The Merseyside Marauders," Stevie answered.

"The Merseyside Marauders! What kind of name is that? Oh, my goodness, this is really bad! And I mean bad!" responded an angry Josh.

"I'll tell you more later," soothed Stevie. "Let's just enjoy the present. We're here at the Etihad and we're beating Man. City 1-0. It's fantastic so let's enjoy the moment. Remember, if you execute your mission in the past then JJ will never be born, and never be able to ruin the last day of the season. So all this future nightmare will be just that... a future nightmare; a bad dream! Man. City will win the league like they should, in the greatest dramatic game which creates such interest that the Premier League greatly strengthens its image and safeguards its future. All that had been undone by Man. Utd completely dominating and Man. City completely falling away. People just lost interest at the predictive monotony of it all, so the Premier League was dying. Man. Utd became so huge that not even the London greats could compete, and the powerful USA could sense this and capitalised. They could smell blood, they could smell opportunity, and they took it! The European Leagues were also getting stale and uncompetitive, which made them extremely vulnerable as well. So the USA took charge of it all, restructured, and created the NASL."

Stevie didn't want to say any more for now. He wanted to enjoy celebrating the final few minutes at the Etihad, albeit keeping an eye out for any flailing arms that might threaten to disturb the time watch.

Final whistle: Man. City 0-Liverpool 1. Massive jubilation amongst the Reds' fans, but it was only the first leg. Man. City were a fantastic team, who could still easily spoil the dream, even at Anfield. But as Josh and Stevie left the Etihad, they gave themselves up to enjoying the precious feeling of victory.

Footnote

Stevie's watch was under an invisibility cloak so as not to arouse suspicion or envy, it was only visible to the wearer (and Josh).

The 25th and 28th January 2012 (Anfield Week)

This was going to be a magical week for Stevie and Josh Stanton. Two massive games at the magical arena of Anfield would provide the chance for Stevie to experience the ultra-special sensation of being in the Kop in ultra-special matches. Liverpool were playing Man City in the 2nd leg of the League Cup, where they had an enormously precious 1-0 cushion going into this tie and a Wembley final the massive prize awaiting. After that there was just the small matter of an Anfield home game against Manchester United in the FA Cup 4th round. What an absolute dream week in store, should Liverpool do the business!

It was certainly an absolute dream for Stevie as he and Josh arrived at Anfield with massive anticipation! Stevie couldn't wait to enter the ground and enjoy the pre-match atmosphere, especially the signature rendition of *You'll Never Walk Alone*, which he knew was going to be sung with gusto and pride. It was so exciting!! The Kop stand looked amazing as Stevie viewed it from the street. How brilliant to be here and experience it for himself!

Josh and, in particular, Stevie were in football heaven as the kick off approached and the Anfield Stadium was pulsating. A seismic wall of noise from the Kop was emanating into a deafening crescendo when *You'll Never Walk Alone* was played over the tannoy and sung with feverish pride by the heaving masses, their red scarves and flags held proudly aloft. It made the goose pimples on Stevie's neck spread out at an enormous rate. He had goose pimples everywhere! This had been one of the prime reasons for him coming back. He'd desperately wanted to experience this ultimately poignant moment, which came a close second to wanting to see his dad again – and, of course, the small matter of trying to help him save the world!

Stevie knew it was going to be a tense but great night as he and Josh joined in with the famous anthem You'll Never Walk Alone in such a cauldron of passion.

As the match kicked off to a tremendous din, Liverpool started on the front foot, displaying a welcome response to a very poor 3-1 defeat and performance at Bolton Wanderers where King Kenny, their manager, had had very harsh things to say. Liverpool were being very positive in their efforts to put the tie out of reach of Man. City. The Reds were in the ascendancy and looking close to scoring and making their life a bit easier, but against the run of play Nigel De Jong curled a spectacular strike into the top corner. Liverpool 0, Man. City 1, and the Kop was stunned into a momentary silence. Anfield was suddenly a worried place, except for Stevie who had a very good idea how it all unfolded.

He knew something good or fortunate was going to happen just before half time and wanted to keep away from too much celebratory madness, to protect his time watch.

"Dad, I'm just going downstairs to the men's room," he said.

"Ok, but it's nearly half-time. We might get lucky and score, and you'll miss it," Josh replied.

Stevie winked at his dad and responded, "We're going to score, but don't worry I'll see it from downstairs, out of harm's way."

He proceeded to make his way downstairs just as Liverpool were awarded an outrageous penalty for what was perceived to be a handball against Micah Richards, when a shot from Agger ricocheted against his arm via his foot. What a stroke of luck! The referee decided it was a penalty, and Steven Gerrard coolly beat Joe Hart with power and placement... Liverpool 1, Man. City 1.

The Reds' fans were mightily relieved as the half time whistle blew, and Stevie reappeared to join Josh. He explained his reluctance to be vulnerable to too much shoving and pushing, even if it meant missing the celebrations.

"Don't take this the wrong way, Stevie, but I hope you have to go downstairs again," Josh laughed.

"I know what you mean," Stevie replied, "and maybe you'll see me do just that in the second half."

Liverpool began the second half as they had the first, exerting tremendous pressure on the Man. City goal, and Joe Hart was forced to be at his brilliant best in the City goal with two magnificent saves. Liverpool were enjoying total supremacy, when footballing disaster struck. Man. City retook the lead against the run of play, through Djeko! Surely the prize of a first Wembley final since the tragic cream-coloured suits of 1996 wouldn't be allowed to slip from Liverpool's grasp? But now it was Liverpool 1, Man. City 2, and Anfield was riddled with anxiety.

"Oh no! I don't believe this!" Josh said forlornly. "I think the Wembley dream is slipping away!"

"I think it's time for me to go downstairs again," Stevie replied.

Josh's spirits were instantly revived at Stevie's remark, and his hope turned to unbridled joy and relief as Craig Bellamy supplied an exquisitely delightful finish past Joe Hart. Liverpool 2, Man. City 2! There were mass celebrations at the Kop end, but there was still the concern that their joy could be shattered, and Liverpool survived a scare late on when a certain brilliant striker by the name of Sergio Aguero almost broke their hearts with a 12-yard shot which was saved by Reina.

The final whistle blew to mass hysteria and delirium. Josh was incredibly joyful as he caught up with Stevie and gave him a big hug. "We're on our way to Wembley!" sang an exceedingly jubilant Josh.

"I know, and I think it's going to be brilliant as well," Stevie replied.

His first Anfield experience had been magnificent, and it was all to come again very quickly as Manchester United were visiting at the weekend in the FA Cup 4th round.

Josh and Stevie again had a fantastic experience, and Josh was loving the sight of Stevie disappearing downstairs as it was a sign of only one thing – an impending Liverpool goal! Stevie was to disappear twice during this game – once just before the 21st minute, as Daniel Agger made it Liverpool 1, Man. Utd 0; then five minutes before the end, when it was 1-1 and a replay looked likely, but Dirk Kuyt took advantage of a David De Gea mistake and hesitation to make it Liverpool 2, Man. Utd 1 in front of an exultant Kop. Liverpool had knocked Manchester United out of the FA Cup. What an absolutely fantastic week to be a Liverpool fan!

A truly special, precious week was going to turn into a truly special, precious month for Josh and Stevie, as their social and football odyssey continued. The highlight of early February would see an away trip to Manchester United at their mighty impressive theatre of dreams, the magnificent Old Trafford.

As Josh and Stevie made their way to the ground, approaching Salford Quays and the Manchester Ship Canal, they took in the breath-taking splendour of Old Trafford in all its glory. This was going to be an extremely interesting match, as Liverpool's Luis Suarez and Man. United's Patrice Evra had been involved in an alleged racial incident in the league match played at Anfield earlier in the season. Suarez was returning after an eight-match ban, so today's encounter was going to be very interesting.

As Josh and Stevie made themselves at home amongst the raucous army of away fans situated in the corner of the east stand and the main south stand, it wasn't long before the controversy began – even before a ball had been kicked. Luis Suarez refused to shake Patrice Evra's hand, provoking outrage in the stadium and especially amongst the Manchester United players. It was all kicking off!

Josh and Stevie were loving the pressure cooker atmosphere of this fierce match, which was exacerbated by Suarez aggressively kicking the ball into the crowd at half time, causing further unrest and aggravation with the Manchester United players and fans. This match was well and truly all about Luis Suarez! Unfortunately, though, it fired Manchester United up and within five minutes of the second half, Wayne Rooney had scored twice. It was Man Utd 2, Liverpool 0.

Stevie disappeared downstairs near the end, just before Liverpool got a goal back – and it just had to be from a certain Luis Suarez! But it was just a consolation, as Man. Utd won and celebrated their 2-1 victory. Josh and Stevie were disappointed, but they had enjoyed a fierce day out at their great rivals, and there were now only two weeks to go to the fantastic prospect of the League Cup final against Cardiff City. Happy days! Precious days!

February 26th, 2012: Wembley League Cup Final Day

The last two weeks had seemed like an eternity, but now the incredible day had arrived. It was League Cup Final day and was time to experience the truly wonderful magic of the iconic Wembley Stadium with its magnificent arch reaching gloriously over the magical arena; the arena of heroes; the stage of legends; the stadium where dreams can come true, but one where plenty of tears are shed.

Josh was full of optimistic bravado but was mindful not to be too complacent. Stevie was reassuringly at ease but giving nothing away as they walked down Wembley Way. The prospect of playing Cardiff City in the final should have been straightforward, with respect, but a Wembley final is where dreams are made and broken, so there was nothing straightforward about this match.

Stevie gave Josh a tantalising clue of what was to come. "Dad, I hope you are going to make sure you've had a good dinner, as you might be here longer then you think," was his cryptic teaser. Josh knew then he was going to be in for an anything but a straightforward day. It sounded like there would be a roller-coaster ride of emotion. *Bring it on, but please let it have a good ending!* he thought. *Please!*

As Josh and Stevie stood with the Liverpool fans allocated in the west end of Wembley Stadium, there was a rude awakening. Horror of horrors, Cardiff City took a shock lead (Liverpool 0, Cardiff City 1) through Joe Mason in the first half, and it was the same score as they approached the hour mark. It was getting very frustrating for everybody, and Josh was looking at Stevie, longing for him to disappear downstairs as a sign of positivity. Then… hallelujah! Stevie made his move, leaving Josh braced with expectation. Joy and relief weren't long in coming, as Martin Skrtel equalised: Liverpool 1, Cardiff City 1.

The match meandered to a tame end, so it was extra time. Again, the first half had little incident, but soon as the second half kicked off, Stevie exited, leaving Josh incredibly excited as he visualised the long-awaited breakthrough and it happened – Dirk Kuyt scored! Liverpool 2, Cardiff City 1.

Stevie returned. *Surely it's now as good as won*, Josh thought. *Cardiff must be so tired and deflated, and there's not much time left. Surely it's Liverpool's cup?*

He turned to Stevie and said, "This is going to be fantastic watching Liverpool go up to get the cup! It's going to be great watching Steven Gerrard hold the cup aloft. Won't be long now!"

"I'm afraid you're going to have to wait longer than that," Stevie replied, noting Josh's shock and deflation.

"You mean Cardiff get a late equalizer and send us to penalties? Oh, my goodness, I hope you're wrong – but you never are," Josh responded with alarm.

And Stevie wasn't wrong. Cardiff sensationally equalised two minutes before the end of extra time and sent the teams to a penalty shoot-out. Liverpool's fans and players were absolutely gutted, being so close to victory. How were they going to raise themselves for this lottery of a penalty shoot-out; Cardiff could cause a sensational upset!

It was an unbelievably worst-case scenario as the penalty shoot-out proceeded and Steven Gerrard missed the first penalty! But then relief, as Cardiff missed as well.

"Phew, my heart can't take this!" complained Josh.

Charlie Adam then missed, and Cardiff scored, so 0-1 to Cardiff.

"Oh no, I can't believe this!" Josh was horrified.

Kuyt scored for Liverpool, then Cardiff missed.

Downing made it 2-1 to Liverpool, but Whittingham scored his penalty for Cardiff to make it 2-2.

All square and all to play for. The nervous tension within Josh's heart was at fever pitch, as Johnson stepped up for Liverpool.

"Please score, please score!" implored Josh, and Johnson duly obliged.

With the penalties score now at 3-2 to Liverpool, it was Antony Gerrard – cousin of the mighty Steven – to take Cardiff's next attempt. He had to score, or it was all over.

As Josh held his breath – along with thousands of other fans in the stadium – Anthony Gerrard missed, and Liverpool had at last won the League Cup!

The joy and the ecstasy of the Liverpool fans was incredible after such a nerve-racking roller-coaster ride, and Josh felt like an emotional wreck. But this was football heaven, and the special centrepiece of this precious occasion was sharing it with Stevie.

There was only about 10 weeks to go, and Josh knew he would miss Stevie. Their time together was proving blissful in the extreme, but there was the undeniable heartstring pull on Josh with the growing anticipation of seeing Emma Chambers again. How on earth was he going to control his emotions when he saw Emma for real again? He knew he had an absolutely heart-breaking mission to perform, and somehow had to summon the strength to resist his natural love for her. Josh honestly didn't know if he was capable or strong enough to resist her, and the apprehension was growing.

He was only going to get one chance. He simply had to resist, and break Emma's heart – and his own at the same time. It was going to be a massive and daunting challenge.

March 2012, Liverpool v Everton (Merseyside Derby)

There was one major event Josh and Stevie hadn't experienced together, and that ambition was fulfilled on March 13th, 2012. A Tuesday night, blood and thunder Merseyside derby between Liverpool and Everton was something that had to be experienced and Stevie knew this was going to be special for one major reason – this was going to be Steven Gerrard's derby. Stevie had been named after Josh's favourite player of all time, Steven Gerrard, so this was going to be a truly special night under the lights.

Josh didn't have to far to travel, and it was always surreal living in Gladys Street, right behind Everton's ground, when there was a Merseyside derby going on at Goodison Park. As his house was situated right behind their most passionate, vocal fans, it was always a stunning conundrum for such a committed Reds supporter, and surreal walking around Goodison Park to the far away end, near Stanley Park, while his house was right behind the home end!

Tonight, however, the match was at his beloved Anfield, so Josh could have a late tea, relax, pass Goodison Park, and take a leisurely stroll through Stanley Park to the mecca that is Anfield, along with a multitude of fans both red and blue, such was the close proximity of each club to the other. The affability of each set of fans was admirable, indeed Liverpool v's Everton was always known as the friendly derby.

Liverpool's fans certainly enjoyed this derby as their team strolled to a 3-0 win, but this match was a particular triumph for a certain Steven Gerrard, who got all three goals for a super hat trick. This was the ultimate joy for Stevie as he joined in the tumultuous singing of Steven Gerrard's chant. The grateful Liverpool fans adored their idol and had dedicated a very strong anthem that Stevie had always sung, even in the far future of 2045. This was an extremely poignant moment and tears of emotion filled Stevie's eyes as he, Josh, and the Liverpool masses, belted out:

> Steve Gerrard Gerrard
> He'll bust 'em from 40 yards
> He's Scouse and he's f(e)cking hard
> Steve Gerrard, Gerrard

It was all too much for Stevie, and he burst into tears of emotional happiness; he had experienced his ultimate football moment!

Josh and Stevie carried on enjoying their football in the time they had remaining, but football had reached its zenith that night, watching Liverpool beat Everton 3-0 with a Stevie G hat trick. That was unbeatable!

The next day, Josh had a big day at Manchester College, as Mr Xavier Richardson was expecting a guest lecturer who excelled in the laws of time and motion, so he couldn't afford to stay up too late celebrating the victory.

Josh had a hard job reducing his super-high levels of adrenalin to try and get some good sleep and was heavy-eyed the next morning when he arrived to encounter an ashen-faced Mr Richardson.

"What's the matter, sir?" Josh was worried at how pale and anxious his friend looked. "Are you alright? It looks like you've seen a ghost."

"I've just found out the name of our guest lecturer, Josh," he replied. "It's... it's... she... Rossi! I think I might have to give this lecture a miss."

"Why on earth do you have to do that, sir? She's probably a lovely lady and I think you'll probably think the same, especially as Stevie has said you'll marry her one day," teased Josh gently.

"That's what I am afraid of," Mr Richardson remarked. "I don't want to think she's lovely, I am happy as I am with no complications."

"But why, sir? With respect, this is silly. You've got to pull yourself together. You can't just avoid a lecture because you're afraid," said Josh, unable to hide his exasperation with his tutor friend.

Mr Richardson sighed. "You're right, Josh, you're totally right. I mean, I would probably need to see her a few times before I had any danger of falling in love. I'm being very silly, aren't I? How dangerous can it be for me to see Miss Rossi?" he continued, sounding far from convincing.

"Exactly. What can go wrong in one day?" remarked Josh. "I can't believe you are afraid of true love, though, it's not as though you have experienced it; you said you never have."

"I have a confession for you, Josh. I didn't tell you the whole truth in my car that day. Once upon a time I did fall in love, when I was young, and I did experience what you describe as true love and felt what you described, the total exhilaration, the heart racing, the butterflies, the floating on air, the total taking over my mind to the detriment of everything else. Even when I was trying to relax or trying to sleep, I had images of this girl incessantly on my mind," Mr Richardson admitted.

"That's wonderful, sir, so why are you so keen to avoid true love?" Josh asked.

"She broke my heart," his friend replied sadly. "She didn't feel the same ultimately, though not before she had given me false hope and allowed me to dream about her night and day and left me helpless to her every whim. She sent out all the signals that she was interested, and then she wasn't. I was in love and got badly hurt; I thought it was mutual true love, as I could feel the electricity in my heart crackle every time I saw her, and I honestly felt someone capable of having that effect on me would feel the same. I saw her smile at me, and the very way she looked longingly at me, felt brilliant. But it wasn't real, and I felt tremendous pain in my heart, it literally ached very badly. I don't want to feel that pain again. I felt violated, actually, so I just don't trust true love, I'm afraid. I've learnt to put up a big shield to protect my heart, so yes, I'm afraid of true love. It can really hurt you," Mr Richardson said with a searing candidness that left Josh in no doubt of his unsettled feelings.

"Thank you, sir, for being so honest, but you can't let one unfeeling girl spoil your whole life. Don't let her have that satisfaction," Josh urged, concerned at the hurt in his friend's voice. "You are a fantastic person, and probably twice the person she will ever be.

"Thank you, Josh, it's very kind of you to say that. She was extremely cute, though. She had that special magic; she was special. I don't like talking about her as it makes me incredibly sad and forlorn even now. I really loved her so much and am gutted she didn't feel the same. I've tried so hard to imagine the worst of her, to try and picture her as ugly, a loser, or a terrible person not worthy of me, but the truth is she's out of my league – she always was and always will be. She's special, no matter how hard I try to convince myself otherwise," said a very pensive Mr Richardson.

"That is so sad, sir, but this Isabella Rossi might just be the lady that stops you forever mulling over someone who's hurt you so badly," Josh suggested. "Love is extremely precious, sir, embrace it when it comes along as it might not come again for a long time. Remember how love can make the world go around and spin on its axis? Don't reject love, it can be the most wonderful thing that you will ever experience, trust me!"

"You're right, Josh. I've calmed down now. If love happens, it'll happen, so there's nothing to be gained by being uptight. Thank you, my friend." At that, Mr Richardson seemed calmer as he waited the arrival of his guest lecturer, Isabella Rossi, and vowed to be the model of decorum and composure.

It was now 10am, and Isabella Rossi was due any minute to give her lecture. Mr Richardson was looking very nervous as he kept looking at his watch, then a smart car pulled up outside and an attractive brunette got out and proceeded to make her way inside the college. Josh Stanton had noticed all this through his window, and quickly warned Mr Richardson.

"She's here, sir, and I have to tell you she looks hot!" teased Josh. "Beauty and brains, what a combination!"

"Josh, you're here to learn from her, not gawp at her. Show her your respect and give her your full concentration, please," Mr Richardson said sternly.

"I will certainly be doing that, sir! No problem there!" Josh smirked. "No problem at all!" He paused briefly. "Will you be sitting in on the lecture, as you implied that you wouldn't be, sir?"

Mr Richardson was just about to confirm that he wouldn't be, when the door opened and in stepped Isabella Rossi. She gave Mr Richardson a friendly greeting and a pretty smile that could hypnotise any male pulse within 20 yards. *Who would want to pass up the opportunity to be friends with such an alluringly beautiful lady with such magnetic attraction?* Josh thought. He knew he shouldn't, but he couldn't take his eyes off from her; she had perfectly long legs and the cutest bum. It was taking all his willpower not to stare. *Mr Richardson, you are one lucky man, if Stevie is correct,* he thought.

"Hello, Mr Richardson, will you be staying when I give my lecture?" asked a friendly Isabella.

"I-I-I think I will be for at least the start," stammered Mr Richardson, struggling to maintain his composure. "It would be rude not to hear what you have to say on time and motion, wouldn't it?"

"That'll be lovely. I can count on your moral support, then can I? I'm a bit nervous when I speak, so it would be appreciated," a grateful Isabella replied.

"Of course, we can't have you feeling nervous, can we?" Mr Richardson was melting already. He was almost like putty in her hands, his famous stoic resolve no match for the magical qualities of this delightfully alluring woman.

Mr Richardson was a picture of helplessness as Isabella delivered a high-quality lecture of intriguing theories to a very appreciative class.

When the lecture finished, she gave Mr Richardson another warm smile. "Thank you for staying for my entire lecture, I really appreciate that."

"Oh, it was... it was... a pleasure, an honour, you were very good," Mr Richardson said, nerves betraying the decorum he was trying to protect.

"Oh, Mr Richardson, you flatter me," she laughed. "Thank you, it's been a pleasure to be here today. Maybe we'll meet again one day as I'm moving to Sheffield College to lecture full time. Perhaps I'll get to be a guest again, you never know, it's not far away. You've made me feel very welcome, and I am very grateful that you gave me a support. I love supportive men, so I do hope it's not the last time we meet," she teased.

"I certainly hope so, too," Mr Richardson replied, "and thank you for coming. It's been a pleasure to meet you."

As Isabella left the room, Josh couldn't help noticing the effect already just one meeting with this special lady had had on Mr Richardson.

"Sir, can I make an observation?" Josh asked.

"What would you like to point out?" Mr Richardson answered, as he stood staring out of the lecture room watching Isabella return to her car.

"Your pupils have dilated massively, sir, are you alright?" responded Josh.

"Impossible! It's your imagination, Josh," Mr Richardson said dismissively, trying to return to some semblance of normality. But inside, he knew he was struggling to counter the massively overwhelming powerful drug that is the onset of love. It was a battle that he was going to find extremely hard to resist, and similar to the battle that was awaiting Josh in Marlow in 1990. Josh knew he had to win his battle for everyone's sake, not least Emma's. His battle against true love was a true love that was never supposed to be shared by those two people at that point in time. At least Mr Richardson and Isabella Rossi wouldn't have that complication, should love and time reach its natural conclusion.

Mr Richardson could protest all he wanted, but his comfortable, non-threatening existence, free from the perils of true love, was now under severe threat. His life was destined to take a different course, one of marriage and fatherhood had been predicted. *Poor Mr Richardson,* thought Josh, *your safe carefree life is going to change, but it might be the most fantastic change. Let's hope so!*

Resume of the Period, January 2012-May 2012

This was definitely the calm before the storm – a delightfully placid period of enjoying everything that was precious. It brought together father and future son to enjoy precious times; it brought unforgettable football memories to be remembered fondly for years to come; it brought the tantalisingly scary prospect of a future romance for a reticent Mr Richardson and the early blossoms of his long dormant heart being sprung back into life. This was a calm, golden period, but it was nearing its end. Action had to be taken soon to protect everybody from a very bleak future which was inevitable should things go wrong. This period had proved that relationships are precious, love is precious, joy is precious, but above all, time is precious.

CHAPTER 7

LET ME SHOW YOU
THE WORLD IN MY EYES

May 13th, 2012 (1 day before D-Day, 1 day before Man. City v QPR)

The storm was now approaching with rapid haste. It was the night before the tumultuous day when Josh Stanton would take a momentous journey to the past, where he would see the enchanting Emma Chambers again. He would be going forward to the past to see his great love and try and shatter her love for him. Tomorrow was also the day Josh would get his first and only brief sight of JJ (Josh Junior) causing untold trouble at a very big football match.

It had been extremely hard being told that poor JJ had been so unfortunate. JJ wasn't to blame for being a victim of circumstance; it wasn't his fault. It was Josh's fault and he knew he had to take full responsibility for this. Meddling with the natural order of time was an extremely reckless act of stupidity, and poor JJ had suffered the consequences. Besides being anxious, Josh was feeling very guilty.

When Stevie came round to see Josh, he could sense how low his dad was feeling. He could feel his guilt and despair, and his apprehension. There were ominous signs that Josh was far from being in the right mindset to properly execute his mission the next day. He needed his spirits greatly uplifted, plus a reminder – a visual reminder – of what was at stake.

Stevie had a surprise for Josh. "Here, I've got a gift for you," he said as he proceeded to give Josh a strange, glowing patch. It was like a miniature glowing orb.

"What's this?" Josh asked. "What am I supposed to do with this?"

"You place it in the middle of your forehead. It is a visual sensory displayer, or a V.O.D for short. It is going to give you images in the future that are seen by me – visions from my perspective – and will imprint them into your visual cortex via this displayer, through its position in the middle of your forehead. It's like your camcorders and mobile phones being played back to you, but it is coming from the future not the past and is showing you what will happen and what might or might not happen, depending on how successful you are tomorrow. It is very personal, and some images will make you smile but some are troubling. Both are to try and give you purpose and motivation for tomorrow," Stevie explained.

"That's great, but isn't it very dangerous for me to have too much insight into the future? Won't this cause the very problems I'm going to the past to correct? Isn't there a danger of time contamination with all this?" Josh looked concerned.

"Don't worry," Stevie replied. "If you execute everything in the past, all you are about to see will be forgotten so there will be no contamination. All this is for now, and the only sign of this experience will be an imprint in your subconscious mind. It will lay very deep within it, so you won't willingly be doing anything untoward. You will get instincts and gut feelings you can't explain, but that is normal; everybody gets instincts and gut feelings. It is your subconscious mind at work when it does this. There is lots of information that is stored there that you are not conscious of, or aware of certain feelings, but they appear in the form of instinct and gut feelings, and that is what you'll feel about certain things in your future."

"Does that explain certain feelings I've had all my life?" Josh asked. "I have had weird sensations, visual sensory stimulations, weird feelings, and they were inexplicable."

Stevie nodded knowledgeably. "It is all the work of your subconscious mind. It filters everything you need to know into your conscious mind, but then stores everything else and keeps it hidden. Sometimes these hidden images can escape the subconscious mind, leaving you with images that you aren't supposed to see, or have feelings that you are not supposed to feel." He looked closely at Josh. "Is there something troubling you, Dad?"

"I do have a sense of living before this life," Josh admitted. "I've had certain enhanced feelings of being a young lady in the Far East, like Korea, and having an accident in a river."

"That's reincarnation," Stevie answered. "What made you think you had an accident in a river?"

"The fact that I used to scream totally irrationally when I was very young having my hair washed. Having water poured all over my face and head provoked hysteria, plus I had a deep overwhelming fear of swimming in the deep end of my local baths when I was young; a totally over-the-top hysteria. It sounds like a message from my sub-conscious protecting me or warning that water can be very dangerous, and I have learned that the hard way," Josh explained.

"Yes, it is very strange how people have thoughts of reincarnation or alien abductions. If you have experienced anything, it will be stored in your subconscious," Stevie replied. "But it's time to stop thinking too deeply. Just put this V.S.D on your forehead and relax, then tell me what you see.

Josh agreed wholeheartedly, not wanting to feel disturbed any more. He put the visual sensory displayer on his forehead and it automatically locked on.

"Tell me what you see, are you getting any images?" Stevie asked. "Remember, it's from my perspective."

"Yes, I'm seeing images. I'm seeing you being picked up as a baby, and... oh, that must be Donna Taylor, the person you say I meet and marry. Wow, she's gorgeous!"

breathed Josh with excitement. "I've done very well, I must say. She's so beautiful with her blonde hair. She is a lovely mum."

"Now what?" pressed Stevie.

"I see me watching you ride your bike for the very first time at the park, I see myself teaching you to swim at the local baths, I see myself playing tennis with you, and watching you play junior football with a local team, and picking up a best player trophy as you score a great goal and are mobbed by your delighted friends. I see myself and Donna taking you on what seems like great holidays; it looks like we're in Florida and, oh, that's Salou, isn't it? I see you watching me and Donna holding hands and... Oh, I'm sorry, we shouldn't have been doing that. Ooops! What I see is happiness and joy, I see love all around and can tell you were having a happy childhood, weren't you?" Josh was transfixed by the images.

"That's right, you were a fantastic dad, and my mum is also brilliant," Stevie said. "I wanted you to see this. Now what do you see?"

Josh swallowed hard. "I see Donna crying her eyes out, I see Anfield being bulldozed, I see no Goodison Park from our street but new houses being built, Stanley Park being cordoned off while they build a new stadium on the park. I see Donna going to see your new senior school teachers, but it's just Donna, there is no sign of me now anywhere. I must have disappeared, is that right?" Josh asked.

"Yes, we were totally devastated. My mum was distraught and cried for months," Stevie explained sadly. "She loved you and took a long time to recover. Now what do you see?"

"I see you with a girl. She's pretty, was she your girlfriend?" Josh asked.

"Yes." Stevie smiled. "She was called Stacey Shaw, and she was fit! She was my first love at senior school."

"Now I see you at college. You've followed the same path as me, have you? Oh wow, there's Xavier Richardson and he's got grey hair and, who's that? Is that Gabriella? She looks just like Isabella Rossi, she's a dead ringer for her. You can tell she was her daughter, can't you?"

Josh was totally fascinated and engaged in what he was watching, but Stevie warned everything wasn't rosy.

"The next bit might be difficult, but I hope it makes you realise the importance of tomorrow," he said. "Tell me what you see."

"I'm seeing trouble, lots of trouble. I see a Scottish uprising on TV, I see the border being closed off and no-man's land being created. Oh my goodness, that is shocking! Has this got anything to do with you telling me about the importance of Katie Chambers-Smith? You said she was supposed to be a special envoy, didn't you?" Josh asked.

"That's exactly right! Katie Chambers-Smith would have prevented a devastating deterioration in

Anglo-Scottish relations, as she was thought to have very gifted oratory and diplomatic skills," Stevie explained. "She was expected to be a fast-rising Member of Parliament, believe it or not."

"I'm seeing N.A.S.L. on TV, and it's New York Nightmares against Merseyside Marauders and we're losing 5-1. What a nightmare!" moaned Josh.

"Yes, we were rubbish! We're always near the bottom three. All the American teams are near the top, as they have all the money and power. Even Manchester's Red Devils are constantly in the bottom half nowadays, as are the Madrid Mavericks (formerly Real Madrid). All the European Teams are struggling. It's not much fun forever seeing a team struggle; it's become very soulless!" Stevie sounded disconsolate. "You can see why I was so excited at watching Liverpool with you, can't you? And all those other fantastic matches as well."

"I can absolutely understand!" a shocked Josh answered. "The future of football sucks, it's horrible."

"It's not just football's future that's horrible," Stevie warned. "You are coming very close to the end of my visual sensory displayer's material. What are you seeing now?"

"I'm seeing loneliness, people just look so sad and lost. Oh my goodness! Everybody seems totally reliant on their technologies, there's a total lack of communication or interaction between anybody, it seems. I'm not hearing any laughing or talking, everybody looks isolated in their own worlds." Josh couldn't hide the amazement in his voice. "This is so sad to see!"

"That's right," agreed Stevie. "People have lost the ability to speak to each other. There are no shops any more or pubs, everything is so sterile now, and people only exist in their own worlds. There is no natural affection, just selfishness. It's a great irony, isn't it, that the more technology advances, the more people regress backwards? And now people have lost their ability to live freely, the technology has taken over to such an extent that people just can't cope without it; they are totally lost."

Josh nodded. "It was getting like that in my era, people becoming incapable of living without a mobile phone glued to their ear every five minutes, and they were well on the way to becoming slaves to social media. If you ever went on public transport like a train, you could guarantee the majority were totally immersed in their own little bubble. There was very little conversation or engagement. I can fully understand what you're saying about technology."

"It's grim that people are so insular," Stevie remarked. "Don't get me wrong, there have been some amazing technological wonders that have advanced since your day. What can you see now?"

"Wow, I can see trains moving at hyper-fast speed. It looks like they're moving on compressed magnetic air. I see devastation, total and utter devastation! I see panic everywhere, total chaos all around, and people are looking terrified and scared. I'm seeing lightning and earthquakes, volcanic fire and raging, angry seas all around. It looks like the sky and the earth and the sea are all breaking apart at the same time! There's extreme sadness; desperation and extreme sadness. This is too much!" Josh complained.

"This is what the onset of the end of the world looks like, I'm afraid," said Stevie. "This is what awaits us if you don't succeed tomorrow. I'm sorry you have had to see this, but it does concentrate the mind, doesn't it? My mum was experiencing this, so you can sense my intense pain and sorrow. Everybody was experiencing this, it's traumatising." The young man was now in tears as the V.S.D. gave one final image.

Josh said, "That's you with Gabriella, trying out your smart-watch. Mr Richardson and your mum are watching as you initiate the time bubble and it forms around you. They are waving you goodbye and they are crying, especially your mum. She looks devastated, and Mr Richardson is putting his arm around her and trying to console her as you slowly disappear from their view, and that's it…"

The V.S.D. had finished its images, and now gently displaced itself from Josh's forehead and fell on to his lap. Stevie still seemed very emotional.

"I'm going to make things right, Stevie," Josh promised. "I needed all this to give me a kick up the backside. You've done the right thing by showing me all this and I can see why you've allowed me into your world. I won't let you down, Stevie. I'm so sorry you've had to endure all this."

"I know, Dad, I know!" Stevie replied. He tried to shake off his sadness to focus on the more pressing matter that this was their last night together in a period where they could enjoy life free from its consequences. It would be their last night as father and son, and Stevie wanted it to be a celebration of their wonderful times together. Time was too precious to be miserable! It was time to be joyful, thankful and optimistic. As the evening progressed, the two talked about their great adventures.

As midnight drew near, it was time for Stevie to leave and let Josh rest for D-Day; the time for forward travel to the past; the day the smart-watch would become green for active; the day Josh would glimpse JJ for the first and only time; and the day Man. City would play QPR at the Etihad, for the Premier League title! It was going to be a huge, huge day.

When Stevie left Josh's house for the last time, he was both troubled and sad! He had a revelation to share with Josh, a startling revelation that he wanted to wait until the last possible moment to reveal. His dad already had a lot of pressure on his plate and needed to sleep well, as he was going to expand an enormous amount of energy the next day. He certainly didn't need to try and sleep on a bombshell. What was Stevie's startling revelation?

CHAPTER 8

BLUE MOON WEEPING!

May 13th, 2012 (D-Day)

The Match

It was 2.30pm as Josh and Stevie Stanton arrived at an incredibly excited but apprehensive Etihad Stadium. They had managed to get some really good seats in the West Stand which was named after Man. City legend, Colin Bell. It was the main stand which housed the players entrance, and Josh and Stevie were seated just two rows from the pitch, near the halfway line where the tunnel and main dugouts were situated.

Josh Stanton was very impressed. Liverpool were playing in Swansea, but their season in the league had petered out a long time ago, although they did make another Wembley appearance in the FA Cup Final. Josh and Stevie had already more than enjoyed their golden period; they weren't greedy.

For a long time, the utmost focus football-wise had been this Man. City v QPR game, particularly as Man.

City and Man. Utd had for weeks been exchanging the leadership of the league. Josh had to admit that to be present at this game was an absolute privilege, as the titanic tussle between them was coming to an incredible climax. Man. City had the power in their own hands. Win, and there was nothing Man. Utd could do about it, because Man. City had a far better goal difference and both teams were on the same points.

Josh was so happy to be here with Stevie, but at the same time he was very nervous about what was to come. As kick off approached, the teams appeared to a tumultuous roar. A deafening crescendo of noise greeted their heroes, but as the game started and progressed, you could sense apprehension all around, particularly when Man. City didn't make a much hoped-for early breakthrough to settle the nerves. Then news filtered through from Sunderland that Man. Utd had taken an early lead, and it spread like wildfire amongst the legions of City fans. Any hope that Man. Utd would make this day easier for City had gone. Man. City were going to have to do it for themselves, but they were making little headway.

The United score had exacerbated the City fans' anxiety that their team might blow their best chance to win the title in over 40 years. Then, relief and utter joy, as City took a 1-0 lead through Pablo Zabeleta. The title was back on; City were in the driving seat again! The half time whistle blew not long after to a very relieved Etihad audience.

Stevie turned to Josh. "How are you feeling, Dad? Are you enjoying it? Are you enjoying this amazing atmosphere?"

"Yes, it's incredible, isn't it?" Josh replied.

"Are you going to be ready for what is to come? It's going to be dramatic in the extreme in the second half." Stevie smiled. "I'll warn you when the big moment happens so you are prepared, as you will be shocked and emotional."

"Ok, thank you," Josh replied, by now as apprehensive as Man. City's fans.

The second half kicked off and the nervousness was palpable. Surely Man. City would put this game out of the reach to let their fans relax and enjoy the ecstasy of being the champions-elect early? But to an audible gasp of collective horror, QPR absolutely stunned everybody by taking advantage of a defensive mistake to make it 1-1! Man. City fans had dared themselves to dream and it was beginning to turn into a nightmare. Surely Man. City wouldn't blow this golden opportunity. Surely they weren't going to make their fans suffer the ultimate heartbreak, one which would be so devastating they might never recover.

It was now approaching 55 minutes, and Stevie gave Josh the signal that it was time to brace himself for the ultimate incident. Joey Barton was tussling with Carlos Tevez towards the corner of the pitch where Man. City were attacking. When he aggressively shoved Tevez, Barton was sent off but attracted everybody's attention by going crazy and even kicking out at Sergio Aguero. The stadium was in uproar, with everyone focusing their concentration on Joey Barton's crazy demeanour, when suddenly… a middle-aged man with a grey beard came from nowhere, invaded the pitch, and kung fu kicked Aguero in the shins.

Sergio Aguero collapsed to the floor in agony, holding his leg. There was pandemonium all around the stadium. The man was swiftly apprehended by Greater Manchester Police but the damage had been done; the player was in no position to continue and would have to go off! As the middle-aged man with the grey beard was in the process of being escorted off the pitch and down the tunnel by the police, his eyes focused with eagle-like fixation on a horrified Josh Stanton. His gaze was one of sheer menace and cut deep into Josh's soul; the hatred in the man's eyes was tangible.

Josh Stanton was mortified as he turned to Stevie. "Please don't say that is JJ, please," Josh implored.

"I'm sorry but it is," Stevie replied. "JJ is ageing very quickly and very badly and has grown bitter with it. He knew you would be here as his mental awareness would be phenomenally high. I'm so sorry that you've had to witness this scene. I know you wouldn't have wanted to intentionally inflict the trouble you caused by creating a baby out of time, but this is the result that can happen. I'm sorry you've had to realise a very painful truth and that is you don't just mess around with time."

"I'm sorry, so sorry," a devastated Josh murmured. "The poor guy looked about 50 and he was only really nearly 20, and I'm responsible! It was JJ, and I'm so sorry!" Tears ran down Josh's cheeks, he was so ashamed and full of self-reproach. "I don't blame JJ for hating me, he has every right to," Josh went on.

"He's also now turned the tide of football history. Look, they're putting the substitute on, Sergio Aguero won't be coming back on. The point of no return has now been breached," Stevie pointed out.

"I guess JJ, being a Man. Utd fan, sensed the damage he could do by taking out Sergio. It would be a form of compensation, a retribution. What did poor JJ have to lose? The poor lad must have been in turmoil, but at least you tell me his pain won't last too much longer." Josh looked pleadingly at Stevie. "You said he just disappears or fades from existence, doesn't he?"

"That's right, and that's why the smart-watch is set for 6pm. JJ is no longer around at that time, and it's safe to engage the time bubble. You do realise that it is now only just over an hour and a half away? Are you getting nervous?" Stevie asked.

"Yes, I am. I'm too shocked at what I've just seen to be really nervous, as all that business with JJ almost made me forget I was time-travelling again, "Josh replied.

"It's time to re-focus now on what is to come. Let's see how this match plays out now Sergio is off the pitch," urged Stevie.

The match had now resumed and was approaching the last 20 minutes. It was still 1-1, despite QPR playing with 10 men. Man. City were applying fierce pressure with their one-man advantage, in an ever-increasing urgency to get the much-needed breakthrough, when QPR unbelievably broke away and scored a goal which stunned the Etihad Stadium. It was Man. City 1, QPR 2 – an unbelievable and unspeakable situation!

The agony etched on the Man. City fans' faces was there for all to see. City piled pile on the pressure with manic desperation, but to no effect. It was nearing the final minute and the desolation in the stadium was tangible. Those poor, poor City fans! They were becoming resigned to their awful fate and to the tag of the ultimate chokers when, in the way Man. City typically maximise the unbearable torture they can inflict on their tormented fans, they made a breakthrough to equalise through Edin Dzeko. Man. City 2, QPR 2, but it's not enough!

With only one minute of their lingering, flickering dreams left, Mario Balotelli jinked into the QPR area and the ball ran free, but it was cleared by a QPR defender. There's no Sergio Aguero to supply the miracle that was supposed to happen! As the referee blew his final whistle, the Man. City players collapsed to the floor in tears. The title had gone, snatched from their grasp by Man. Utd who by now were wildly celebrating up in Sunderland at the suffering and torment of their rivals. The Utd fans were merciless in their taunting, "Let's all laugh at City, let's all laugh at City. 45 years and you mucked it up (x4). You'll never win it again, you'll never win it again."

Inside the Etihad, grown men were openly in floods of anguished tears, people crying uncontrollably, even the blue moon on the corner screen looked looking like it was weeping!! Those who weren't in tears just stood in a traumatised silence.

Josh and Stevie were finding the deep gloom unbearable as they made their way out of the heartbroken stadium. As they exited, they knew there was serious business to attend to, and all this horrible distress that the Man. City fans were suffering would never happen.

They arrived at their appointed place by the side of Ashton Canal near the Etihad. It was now 17.15 – only 45 minutes to initiation of the time bubble. Just enough time to watch all the distressed fans file out of the stadium towards the city centre in wretched misery. No-one wanted to hang around a scene of desolation, and the area emptied with record speed.

Josh and Stevie had the area almost entirely to themselves as they prepared to spend their last half hour together as father and future son. Half an hour would not take long to come around, and Stevie really wanted to make the most of this very short time they had left. He had something he wanted to say to Josh before he handed over his chronologically temporal-sensitive, super-smart time watch (or smart-watch for short)

COUNTDOWN

As the minutes passed very quickly towards 18.00 hours and time bubble initiation, Josh could sense Stevie was becoming emotional.

"Don't worry, I'll be alright. I know what I have to do. I'm ready as I'll ever be after seeing all that horrible drama played out," Josh reassured him.

"I know you will be but... but..."

"What's up? Are you getting all emotional on me?" Josh tried to lighten the atmosphere a little. "If things work out properly, I'll see you in just over eight years, and hopefully enjoy a future free from calamity, a world where the natural timeline is restored to its natural course. Won't it be much nicer to see the Premier League still being strong? We can watch our beloved Liverpool together at Anfield, and hopefully I won't disappear like I was due to in the other reality. Donna Taylor sounds a very nice lady, and I will no longer have any conscious memory of Emma Chambers, however much I have to admit she's very special. What I don't know can't hurt me, can it? So, I'll be free of longing for someone I wasn't supposed to love in the first place, which I have to admit will be a relief!"

"I know it sounds wonderful, but..." interrupted Stevie.

"But what?" Josh asked. "What is it? What's troubling you so much?"

Stevie's fragile emotional state gave way to a flood of tears as he admitted, "Dad, my future is uncertain, it is unclear whether I'll see you again. When Gabriella was making all those calculations in the future, she could confirm with iron clarity a whole plethora of people and situations would happen or be destined to happen.

She couldn't confirm whether I was supposed to exist or not, so my future is most definitely unclear. It also means you might not necessarily marry Donna Taylor in the future. That has also not been confirmed but nor has it been totally ruled out. You can see why I'm so emotional, Dad, can't you?" Stevie spoke between sobs.

"Spending all this precious time with you again, and the time I spent with you in the future just past (pardon the paradox), has made me realise how much you have meant to me. I love you, Dad. I want to live and enjoy life, but I don't know if I will. It's all up in the air. But I also know that coming back to the past to see you was the greatest privilege and something, if I don't exist again, I will treasure up to the last breath of my existence."

Josh was stunned at Stevie's admission and was extremely emotional as well. This was a massive bombshell to give him just 10 minutes before the initiation of the time bubble. How many shocks could one person take in one day? He watched his grief-stricken son struggling to regain composure.

"Stevie, my son, my adorable son, I want you to know you're the most wonderful son any father could ever wish to have. The last five months have been magical, and even though it's weird that I'm your father (and yet) at this moment in time you're 25 and 6 years older than me, I've come to realise that I love you very much or will come to love very much. I'm confused why your future existence had yet to be confirmed, as everything you showed me on you V.S.D. (Visual Sensory Displayer) was looking fantastic up to the point I disappeared, so it doesn't make sense, no sense at all! Stevie, I want you to know I love you; I want you to know that." Josh was overcome with emotion as he tried to continue.

"Thank you, Dad, that means everything to me."

It was now 17.55, and time for Stevie to remove his smart-watch and pass it over to Josh. As he did so, Stevie warned him, "This will feel really weird for you, because it will give you a massive tingling sensation as it is preparing to go live ready for initiation. You will feel this sensation increasing in ferocity, it'll be like a million ants crawling on your arm, so don't be alarmed. It's normal. At 18.00 hours the watch will glow green and you press this engage button, which will be activating a distorted field around you. That is the time bubble forming around you and enveloping you, then the next thing you know you will be in Marlow 1990. Your smart-watch will only be visible to you when you arrive, due to its invisibility cloak, to protect you from anybody's undue curiosity. The smart-watch will be showing red, and that is showing you that the natural timeline has yet to be restored. If you are successful, you will know because the red will turn to green on your smart-watch."

Stevie went on, "Whatever happens in Marlow, the smart-watch will automatically return you to the present day at midnight, and you will feel yourself sitting back in your seat at the Etihad Stadium as the teams come out for the second half. I won't be sitting next to you anymore, and you won't have the smart-watch on your arm any longer. It will have disappeared. If everything is as it should be, you will see Man. City win the league with a truly sensational winner from Sergio Aguero, then take your life on from there and see where it was supposed to take you."

Stevie cleared his throat nervously. "It is 17.59; time to say goodbye."

The intensity of the smart-watch was now ferocious and causing Josh to wince. It was a good job he had AB negative blood, or he'd be dead by now! The smart-watch was now glowing green, and all Josh had to do was to press engage and the time bubble would form around him. It was time for him to say his final goodbye to Stevie.

"Goodbye, son, I really hope I see you in the future," he said.

"Goodbye, Dad, and good luck. Whatever happens in the future, I want to tell you one last thing," Stevie replied.

"What's that?" Josh asked.

"Thank you for my life, Dad."

Josh blew a fatherly kiss as he pressed the engage button. Immediately, the time bubble enveloped him and all he could make out was Stevie crying and waving a tearful farewell as he faded from sight. Josh's feelings of sadness at this one last lingering sight of his son was exacerbated as he noticed the Etihad Stadium in the distance as he was fading from the scene. Josh could have sworn the blue moon at the Etihad really looked like it was weeping.

Let's hope when Josh returned from his mission in the past, the blue moon would have no reason to be weeping except maybe tears of joy, tears of ecstasy and above all tears of relief at a future restored.

CHAPTER 9

FORWARD TO THE PAST

<u>Wycombe Road</u>

<u>Marlow 1990 (October 1st) 19.00 Hours</u>

Josh looked nervously around as the time bubble dissipated around him, and there he was back in Marlow. He had materialised in the Wycombe Road area, close to the pub where history was going to play out one way or the other. The next few hours were the most important in not only Josh's life but for the whole of mankind. It was the utmost pivotal time in the whole natural timeline. Josh's watch was red as it indicated the confirmed date of October 1st, 1990.

As Josh approached the pub, he took a massive gulp of air. He was so incredibly nervous and his heart was beating fast. Josh could feel the irresistible ache and stomach churn of anticipation at the thought of seeing Emma Chambers alive again, with her magnificent cuteness and magnetic charm. His nerves, though, were caused by his fear that he was going to have trouble executing his mission to break the bond of true love between himself and Emma Chambers. But break it he must.

Entering the pub, he nervously looked around. The place was busy and the quiz had already started. Mr and Mrs Chambers were struggling and looked pleased to see him.

"Come here, Josh, we need your help badly. We're glad you've come," Mr Chambers said.

"Hello, it's nice to see you again. Of course I'll help you," replied a hesitant Josh.

"Good man. Let me buy you a drink," was the friendly response.

In the original past timeline (in 'Stop Mark Robins'), Josh had exchanged longing, loving looks with the beautiful barmaid in almost perfect synchronicity, such was mutual attraction. That was when Josh had decided to take action and pluck up the courage to speak to her, only to see her talking to her childhood sweetheart, Michael, who is now known to be her supposed future husband and father to a certain Katie Chambers-Smith. At that time, the feeling of missed chances had prompted Josh to admit to Emma's parents that he liked her and been informed that Emma had confided in them that she had strong feelings for him, too. Josh had then asked Emma out and expressed his love for her, which was all that Emma had needed to hear. The rest had been tangled history.

All this had made Josh aware that Michael would be coming into the pub in the next 30 minutes, so he would have to act fast. Josh knew he would have to 'blow his chances' with Emma in the next half an hour so that she would be a lot more receptive to hearing what Michael had to say when he arrived. She needed to know that Josh wasn't interested in her as she had thought, but that was the part of the plan which was going to be easier said than done.

Josh turned around to look at the bar, and there she was! Emma Chambers, as beautiful and cute as ever. Noticing Josh's presence in the pub, Emma gave Josh the most warm and enchanting smile. He couldn't help himself responding to such an irresistible, radiant lady. Emma's eyes seemed alive and perked up, and Josh was the same. This was not a good start; not promising at all!

He was in mental agony as he prepared to engage Emma in conversation, knowing this was his one and only chance to alter history in the way it had to be, for everyone's sake. But he was totally in awe of Emma's alluring charm, the power of her femininity, her effortless grace, the infectious *joie de vivre* she could display, how she moved with such a hypnotic sway. Everything about her was perfect in every way, and Josh was spellbound once again. His task was Herculean, and he really didn't want to have to do this when his heart and body yearned for her so much.

The last time Josh had set eyes on Emma, she had drawn her last breath in the hospital, after she whispered the words, "I remember you. I love you, too." That had been in July 2011, under a year ago in that twisting present. And yet here was Emma in 1990, standing on the other side of the bar, just a width and breadth of wood away. She could reach out and touch Josh if she wanted to.

She didn't hide her pleasure as she greeted him. "Hello, it's really nice to see you in here. Are you having your usual half a lager?"

"Yes please, Emma," Josh replied, struggling to get the words out of his mouth as he stood mesmerised like a rabbit in the highlights.

"How are you getting on with my mum and dad?" she asked, as she poured his drink. "It's really nice of you to be helping them with the quiz."

"It's going ok, thanks," Josh replied. "I think we're near the top, as my sports knowledge is helping them and maybe a little music and geography knowledge has helped as well. I like your parents, they're very nice people. In fact," he handed over some money, "your dad very kindly gave me the money to pay for this drink."

Emma beamed. "Oh, that's nice of him. It shows they like you." She rang up the till. "Will you be staying long in Marlow, as you just visit, don't you? I hope you will visit more. Marlow is a beautiful place with lots of fantastic people living here." Her tone was extremely encouraging.

"Thank you, I'm sure I would be very happy here if I could stay. You're so lovely…" Josh immediately recognised his Freudian slip and tried to correct himself. "I mean, it's so lovely. Sorry about that, it was a silly slip of the tongue." He was blushing furiously.

"Hey, don't apologise," Emma laughed. "I am very happy to be called lovely. I think I might have to call you lovely to make us equal," she gushed as she began involuntarily twirling her hair, her interest in Josh patently obvious.

This was all going seriously wrong! Josh was feeling powerless against the overwhelming tide of pure love he was feeling for Emma. The romantic tension and chemistry were so indefinably palpable between them that Josh was fighting a battle he was losing the will to win.

It was approaching the time Michael was due to come into the pub. The world was looking doomed by the power of love, and something badly needed to happen or all future hope would be lost. But just when it looked like there was no way of breaking this terminal bond between them, there was a chink of light.

Emma suddenly noticed a ring on Josh Stanton's left hand and looked troubled. She didn't realise that it was actually the ring she gave to Josh on his seventeenth birthday as a special friendship ring, and which he'd worn ever since.

"Oh, that's a nice ring on your finger, who gave you that?" Her efforts to sound nonchalant didn't work, and Josh could sense this was the absolutely pivotal moment! Would Josh tell Emma it's from her? And if he did, would she find the notion ludicrous? Or would Josh take this God-given, golden opportunity to finally start breaking their bond of love, for the world's sake? It seemed to take him ages to reply as he took in the magnitude of this moment.

"My ring? It's erm… erm… a ring that was given to me by a really special friend up north."

Her face fell as he spoke, but she was still curious. "Oh, do you still see her? So, you really like her? I suppose you must really like her as you are wearing her ring. I feel really foolish but I thought I could sense that you really liked me and I was really liking you…" a far from happy Emma faltered.

"I'm really sorry if you think that, but if it means anything, I do like you—" Josh was in the middle of replying, when Emma cut him short.

"But you are wearing a ring from another woman," she snapped. "I'm sorry but I need to serve other customers. I can't hang around talking to strangers." Emma turned away abruptly, leaving Josh in no doubt that she was miffed.

Josh reckoned Emma had every right to feel miffed! There's nothing worse than thinking or allow yourself to believe that a person you have deep feelings for is not what you think they are. You feel very foolish and hurt, not just as your own stupidity but at the cruelty by the object of your affections.

He felt totally devastated at seeing the hurt in Emma's eyes, and hated himself, but he knew it had to be done. Josh's heart was breaking into thousands of pieces and tears were not far away, but he had to keep his dignity and composure and not give away his true feelings. No sooner had he sat down than Michael came into the pub.

Josh looked at his smart-watch and saw that the red was beginning to fade, meaning time was re-mending and the natural timeline was being restored. He should have been happy and relieved, but his heart was breaking at the greatest love of his life falling out of love with him and maybe even really disliking him.

As the quiz night continued, Josh's heart was no longer in it as he watched Emma and Michael talking intently. Mr and Mrs Chambers had noticed the change in Josh's demeanour and had also noticed their precious daughter's change of mood. All Josh wanted to do now was leave the pub and wait for his smart-watch to engage at midnight; he couldn't wait to initiate the time bubble for return travel to 2012. He'd done all he could in the past and it was very painful, so he didn't want to spend a moment longer there than he had to. The onset of green on his smart-watch couldn't come quick enough.

The last two hours of the past seemed like two days as Josh walked by the River Thames and through the park in a state of sheer distress. His tears now unrelenting in their frequency, Josh wanted his torture to end. It was taking forever to reach the midnight hour.

But then relief was at hand as Josh felt the non-welcome build-up of intensity within his smart-watch. The ferocity signalled the end of his and also the world's nightmare. Josh didn't care that it was hurting. He knew when he re-appeared at the Etihad Stadium in Manchester, his memories of Emma Chambers would reside firmly only in his sub-conscious mind. It was all for the best.

The smart-watch was going live; it was time to leave the past behind.

The Return

May 13th, 2012 4pm Etihad Stadium Manchester

As Josh got his bearings, he could not fail to hear the excited singing ringing in his ears. There was no doubt he was back in the comfort of the Etihad Stadium. The Man. City team had just come out for the second half, and the nervous anticipation was building amongst the Manchester City fans. Josh noticed the empty seat next to him. There was no Stevie, as he'd said there wouldn't be. Indeed, now Stevie was a person instantly buried deep into the subconscious mind of Josh Stanton, as was Emma Chambers.

There was no smart-watch on Josh's arm, it had vanished during his time transit before his materialisation (please see footnote at end of chapter), and again Josh had no conscious idea that he'd ever had a smart-watch or all the adventure that had been undertaken with it in the first place. Josh had no idea whatsoever that he had just helped save the world! There was now no friendship ring on his finger anymore; it had been erased.

Josh Stanton, for all he knew, was here to enjoy the fantastic climax to the Premier League football season and enjoy it he did. He watched all the action unfold as it should: QPR equalised, Joey Barton got sent off, with no unfortunate JJ to mess with football history (again now just a figment of Josh Stanton's subconscious mind); QPR sensationally took the lead until the onset of injury time; Edin Djeko equalised; then the fantastic, sensational moment when Sergio Aguero sent the Etihad Stadium into ecstasy with the winning goal. The Man. City fans had been sent to heaven all the way from hell, and the blue moon wouldn't be seen weeping that night unless it was tears of unbridled joy.

The City fans were in raptures as they belted out their anthem Blue Moon.

Everything was fine, everything was as it should be as the natural timeline had been restored. Everybody could now relax, couldn't they??

Footnote

As the smart-watch was no longer on his arm, there wouldn't be the clearly evident time bubble round him.

It would be a similar effect to the way Josh would be in new surroundings as he stepped out of the time bubble in 'Stop Mark Robins'. It obviously had to be this way <u>deliberately,</u> to avoid startling the many thousands of football fans leading to renewed time contamination. The smart-watch disappeared and dissipated bubble milliseconds before Josh's conscious re-appeared.

CHAPTER 10

MYSTERIOUS WAYS

Summer of 2014, The Present Day

It was July 2014, in the height of summer. It had been two years since that absolutely tumultuous day at Manchester City's Etihad Stadium, the most important day in mankind's history. Josh had absolutely no idea that he had played the pivotal part in making the future as safe as it could be. At least the natural timeline wasn't badly tangled any more, and time could be played out without interference. What will be, will be!

The July day was one of sadness and one of looking forward for Josh Stanton. The reason for sadness was that it was Josh's final day at Manchester College, so he was leaving behind lots of fantastic memories and a certain Mr Xavier Richardson, who had been a very close friend as well as a brilliant tutor. Josh was going to miss seeing Mr Richardson almost daily, but this disappointment was tempered by the knowledge that Mr Richardson was now in the throes of a budding relationship with a certain Isabella Rossi. Against all protestations, Mr Richardson had been unable to resist the urge to keep in touch with Miss Rossi, and it was growing into a beautiful relationship! Poor Mr Richardson, didn't he know that it was futile – even with the most austere heart – that it is nearly impossible to stop the inevitable when confronted with an irresistibly beautiful lady who enchants you?

Josh Stanton was very happy that Mr Richardson was very happy; if anybody deserved this happiness it was Xavier Richardson. Josh also had good reason to look forward, as he was starting an exciting job with a scientific research company in September. And he was going on a 'lads' holiday' to Tenerife tomorrow, along with Ryan Brown (his Evertonian best friend in 'Stop Mark Robins').

Josh had been happily single for the last two years, but this 'lads' holiday' would present a welcome opportunity to see if romance or something more exciting would happen. He knew he had probably been single because he was picky. He hadn't met anyone that rocked his world, someone that could instantly make his goose pimples appear, someone that would make his heart race. And he knew deep down that anything else just wasn't the real thing.

As the lads approached the airport, Josh was coming in for some merciless teasing.

"Hey, Josh, are you ready for this holiday? We're going to find you a nice girl. It's about time you started enjoying the female touch again," Ryan said with mischievous banter.

"We'll see," Josh replied. "We'll see if anybody interests me."

"That's the trouble, Josh, you're far too picky for you own good. Please don't get me wrong, you're a good-looking lad but this high standard stuff is stopping you having fun. There are so many pretty girls out there waiting to meet you, to have fun with, if you're lucky. You are seriously missing out!" Ryan was concerned for his best mate.

"You're probably right, Ryan, I'll try and be less choosy. It's time that I fully enjoyed life again," agreed Josh.

"That's good to hear." Ryan was buoyed up by Josh's rediscovered enthusiasm. "Let's get ready for lots of sand, sea and… Sangria! Nightclubs, here we come!"

History was history, the past was the past, it was time to move on as life was too precious not to! The present and 'the now' was the most important thing, and the future could wait and take care of itself. Josh was realising this slowly, knowing he had to live his life with as much happiness as he could muster. Love, true love, might remain forever elusive so Josh had to move on with his life.

Throughout the holiday. He tried really hard to be as good as his word but something was holding him back that he couldn't explain. The rest of the lads were having a fantastic time drinking and being in the company of delightful ladies, but it was all passing Josh by. By the final night of the holiday, this was definitely becoming a serious case of missed opportunity for Josh.

As Josh stood alone at the bar, his attention was suddenly drawn to a group of girls dancing by the side of the dance floor. Their delightful exuberance was intoxicating, and Josh's eyes had focused on a brunette, a flicker of interest managing to permeate the inertia in his heart. Josh stood increasingly fascinated with this brunette, and as the night went on the urge to talk to her was overwhelming.

He was feeling the butterflies in his stomach as he left the safety of the bar and went over to say hello to the girl. "Hi, I'm Josh, I hope you don't mind but I've been watching you all night and just had to come over and say hello. I think you look amazing." Josh was blushing a brighter shade of crimson, but thankfully the brunette was friendly.

"That's nice of you to say, Josh. You look nice yourself. Are you having a good time in Tenerife?" replied the brunette.

"Yes, I am, but it's just got better, seeing someone like you. I just wish this wasn't my last night," said a gutted Josh.

"That's a pity," said the brunette. "You can hang around with us if you want, as it is your last night?"

"Thank you, I'd love that," answered Josh.

As the night went on, it was obvious that Josh had met someone who had reactivated his heart. He and the brunette were getting on fantastically well and getting to know each other, to the extent that nobody else existed in their world.

"What made you come to Tenerife?" she asked. "Is it a lads' holiday you are on?"

"Yes, what about you? Are you on the same?" Josh asked, realising that he meant a girls' holiday not lads' holiday.

"Yes, it was organised to cheer me up as my dad died a little while ago and I was devastated, as was my mother. So I've really needed this holiday." She looked downcast for a few minutes.

"Oh, I'm really sorry to hear that. I lost my father quite a few years ago, when I was very little, so I can only guess how it feels," Josh responded.

As the night was coming to an end, Josh and the brunette had become closer, and passionate kisses had been exchanged during the obligatory slow dance. It was time to leave. Happiness had come far too late, it seemed, for Josh.

"Can I walk you back to your hotel?" he asked.

"Of course. I'd like that," the brunette answered.

As they neared her hotel, walking hand-in-hand, Josh realised that he wanted to see her again.

"Is there any way we can stay in touch, or maybe see each other again, back in the UK?" he asked, his heart beating nervously as he waited for her reaction. "I really like you."

"I'd love to stay in touch with you," she replied with a beaming smile. "What is your home address?

"Gwladys Street in Liverpool," said Josh. "My house just happens to be right behind Everton's football ground, but I'm a big Liverpool fan so you can imagine the weirdness and irony of where I live, can't you? Do you like football?" Josh wondered if she could be even more perfect than she seemed already.

"I love football, but where I live we're all Arsenal supporters. I have been known to go to the Emirates Stadium occasionally, so I guess it's another thing we have in common, isn't it? Actually, that'll be one way we can keep in touch," she suggested. "I'll watch Arsenal at Anfield and Goodison Park, and you can watch football, and in particular Liverpool, with me at the Emirates. My mum also likes football so we can go together. It'll be great!"

"I think I'm love!" joked Josh, but he wasn't even half joking. He suddenly realised he didn't know where she lived, or incredibly even her name. He had been so absorbed all evening that he hadn't asked the most fundamental question. Josh felt really foolish.

"I know this sounds incredible, but I haven't asked you your name," he said, looking sheepish. "I know so much about you and yet I don't know your name. You're the most fantastic girl I've seen in years…"

The brunette laughed as she finished Josh's sentence for him. "My name is Katie. It's Katie Chambers-Smith."

Summary/Conclusion

It is absolutely incredible how love can move in such mysterious ways. Josh Stanton wasn't aware of it but the lady he was getting very fond of already was (Katie Chambers-Smith) Emma Chambers' daughter! Love always finds a way, but this was an incredible twist. How would Josh Stanton react when, or if, he saw Emma Chambers again? Especially as Josh was developing deep feelings for Katie, her daughter. Would Josh's feelings for Emma be even stronger? Would he find Emma was attracted to him, despite knowing Katie was his girlfriend or at least a very good friend of his? Was Josh always supposed to be with Emma? Who is now available in the right part of the natural timeline to have a relationship with Josh? Or was Josh supposed to meet and be with Katie, Emma's daughter? And what about Donna Taylor, whom he was supposed to meet and marry in the future? Will he ever meet her in the first place? And does that mean poor Stevie will never be born now? Will Josh have a future son at all? Will Josh still disappear in the year 2030?

Yes, love truly does move in mysterious ways!

STAND-ALONE BONUS CHAPTER
THE MIRACLE OF TIME

Set-up Explanatory

When Stevie appeared in the year 2011 (Christmas Eve) in Josh Stanton's bedroom, complete with his smart-watch that had enabled him to travel from the year 2045 (which just happened to be the end of the world), it was made clear that Stevie's smart-watch had been carefully pre-set to operate to a very specific set of conditions, such as being engaged at a specific location on a specific date and time. It was all delicately co-ordinated to enable maximum possible efficiency; all this was the brainchild of future genius, Gabriella Richardson.

It was good to report that everything turned out satisfactorily in the end. The smart-watch operated brilliantly in the intricate way it sent Stevie back to Josh (2045-2011), and Josh back to the past (2012-1990) and gave him return travel back to the present (1990-2012). Indeed, such was the impressive accuracy of the smart-watch that it managed to return Josh a millisecond before automatically disappearing from his arm and leaving its awe-inspiring time bubble around Josh which might, just might, be very noticeable in a packed Etihad Stadium. The match was being watched by billions of people around the world, so it would have been a gigantic own goal for potential time contamination.

In essence, to use one of Mr Xavier Richardson's famous analogies, the smart-watch parachuted Josh back to the Etihad milliseconds before arrival, like a plane drops off a parachutist. The smart-watch was no longer visible anywhere, and most certainly not with Josh, so what happened to it? Where did it go? Was it naturally erased after returning Josh? The answer is no, it wasn't erased. It had another pre-set function to perform, a function put in by Gabriella Richardson and unknown to everyone including Stevie. There was a reason behind this, but it was also going to act as a means of providing an extraordinary gift for Josh Stanton; it was going to temporarily provide a miracle of time. This was going to cause an emotional hurricane for an un-expecting Josh and his mum, Jane Stanton (in the year 2005, as mentioned in 'Stop Mark Robins'). The new co-ordinates on the smart-watch immediately switched themselves into automatic mode as soon as the smart-watch detached itself from Josh's arm (like a plane diverts off to a predestined location once it has dropped off its parachutists). What was the smart-watch's new destination? Where would it re-appear?

The answer was the A580 near Liverpool, just before 18.00 hours on 15th December 1998, and it was going to a very specific car which was driving that day on the A580, at that precise time and location. The smart-watch had been auto-planned to attach and engage instantly onto a driver travelling on the A580 at that time, on his way home to his beautiful wife and young son in Liverpool from a hard day's work. This driver was on his way to Gwladys Street and couldn't wait to see his wife and his incredibly wonderful five-year-old son, who absolutely loved him back.

The driver's name was Peter Stanton – Josh Stanton's much loved and missed father. But Peter Stanton was never going to arrive home that evening! He was seconds away from having his life cruelly taken away in an horrific traffic accident caused by a callous driver who was driving in a totally reckless manner. Peter Stanton was living the last seconds of his life before being tragically killed, and unfortunately nothing could be done to alter this permanently (as proven in 'Stop Mark Robins', it wouldn't have turned out well). However, there was going to be a temporary miracle of time that was going to provide Mr Peter Stanton a brilliant, truly brilliant, going away present. And poor Peter at least deserved that miracle!

Peter Stanton was looking forward to a night at home with his precious family when his relaxed mood swiftly turned to horrified fear as a fast-moving flashy car appeared at tremendous speed on his side of the road, right before a sharp bend. Poor Mr Stanton was inescapably heading for a full-on collision when... What the...? Peter Stanton wasn't to know this yet, but the smart-watch had materialised onto his arm, attached and engaged, instantly transporting Peter to a future time and place. The time in this very present moment had been temporarily frozen as Peter was displaced (like a pause button on a DVD). Where was Peter being taken to and when? (It's lucky he had AB blood like his son.)

Gwladys Street, Liverpool

Date 25th May 2005, Time 21.00 hours

It was a very important night on Merseyside, and everybody it seemed had forsaken the streets a long time ago. Stanley Park had emptied and there was no-one about anywhere. There was a good reason for all this as Liverpool had made the Champions League final against AC Milan. It was Liverpool's first final since the terrible night at Heysel Stadium where human disaster had struck. The last time Liverpool had been European Champions was as long ago as 1984, when they won their fourth trophy. Now they were aiming for their fifth, after a long 21-year wait. Winning the trophy had gained extra importance, as Liverpool had suffered a relatively poor season, and the only possible way they could be in next season's Champions League was to win it. Even then, it was still under discussion; lose, and that was it. To compound the horror, it would be Everton that would take their place, so losing was definitely not an option!

As it approached 9 o'clock and half time in the final, losing was very much what Liverpool were doing. After what can only be described as a disastrous first half, it was AC Milan 3- Liverpool 0, and the match was being watched by a very dejected and disconsolate 12year old Josh Stanton. He was extremely cheesed off at what was looking like a total humiliation! In fact, Josh was very seriously thinking of switching the TV off and going to bed, such was his disgust.

Jane Stanton (his mum) was already upstairs having a relaxed and soothing hot bath, without a care in the world. But all this was soon to change as there was a knock at the door.

"Josh, there's someone at the door. Can you see to it, please? I don't know who would want to call at this time of night," Jane shouted down.

"Ok, Mum, don't worry," Josh responded, and got up and headed to the front door. The football was definitely not interesting him much, so he didn't care who was knocking.

As Josh opened the door, he was in for an absolutely bone-shaking shock when he was greeted by the visitor; it was his dad, Peter Stanton, standing at the front door! His dad, who had been dead for over six years, killed in a car accident on the A580.

Josh couldn't speak. He was in a state of total and utter shock, as was his dad at seeing Josh as a 12-year-old boy and not the lovingly cute five-year-old Mr Stanton had said goodbye to in the morning with a massive hug and kiss.

They both stood dumbfounded, staring at each other, until Josh's mum shouted down, "Who is it, Josh? Have you sorted it?"

Eventually, Josh found his voice. "Mum, I think you need to come down"

"Oh Josh, can't you sort it?" His mother sounded irritated. "I'm really enjoying my relaxing bath, can't it wait?"

"Trust me, Mum, it can't wait. You need to come down as soon as possible, trust me," implored Josh.

There was a loud sigh. "Alright, I'll be down in a minute," she shouted down. "It had better be a good reason or you'll be in trouble, Josh.

Josh didn't reply. He knew there was no chance of his mum being disappointed at being asked to interrupt her relaxing bath. In the meantime, his dad was trying to get his bearings. Surely there must be a sensible explanation somewhere, somehow?

"Hello, Josh, can I come in?" Mr Stanton asked, not really knowing why he had to ask. It was his house, wasn't it?

"Of course, come in," replied a still very shocked Josh.

"What are you watching on TV, Josh?" asked Mr Stanton, realising that there was a football match going on.

"It's the Champions League Final, Dad. Liverpool versus AC Milan and they've just started the second half, but we're 3-0 down and playing like—" Josh didn't have the chance to finish his sentence as

Mr Stanton moved quickly into the room, looking at the TV in total amazement.

"Liverpool in the Champions League Final? But it's the middle of winter (Mr Stanton died in December 1998). It's Christmas in less than two weeks," he said. "And why you are so tall?"

"Dad, please sit down. I don't know what's happening but watch the match with me and I'll tell you what I know. Mum will be down any minute now as well," Josh said, becoming more concerned.

Mr Stanton sat himself down just as Liverpool scored through a Steven Gerrard header. It was AC Milan 3, Liverpool 1.

"Get in!" roared Mr Stanton, momentarily forgetting his predicament.

"Yes, c'mon!" agreed Josh.

And the situation was soon made even better as Smicer supplied a good finish to make it AC Milan 3, Liverpool 2.

"Yes, yes, yes! C'mon, we can do this!' shouted Josh, pulsating energy.

"We can do this. Yes, c'mon you Reds!" roared Mr Stanton in full agreement.

Then, unbelievably, the Reds were awarded a penalty.

"It's a penalty! Yes, the referee's given it!" Josh yelled, dancing around the room.

"Calm down, Josh," said his father. "He's got to score it first.' Mr Stanton was by now totally absorbed in the match. He didn't know what was going on or how, but this was out of this world! A totally mind-blowing experience!

"Oh no! It's been saved!' wailed Josh. "No, wait a minute, Xabi Alonso's put the rebound in. Yesss!"

It was now AC Milan 3, Liverpool 3; unbelievable. Both Josh and Mr Stanton were now going totally crazy, dancing like mad men all around the living room just as Jane Stanton made her way downstairs.

"This had better be worth it!" Jane opened the living room door and almost fainted with total shock. "Peter! Oh my God!" Her unbridled elation was tempered with horrified realisation. "You're not supposed to be here!"

"What do you mean, I'm not supposed to be here?" her husband replied. "I live here. You're looking at me like you've seen a ghost!"

Jane burst into tears as she put her arms around Peter and squeezed him for all she was worth.

"How did you get here tonight?" she asked.

Peter shook his head. "Do you know, that is a very good question. I was driving along the A580 coming home to you, and the next thing I know I'm standing in the middle of Stanley Park with this fancy watch on my arm showing the figure 110 in the middle circle. I walked to our front door and Josh answered it but he's no longer a five-year-old boy. Can you explain it?"

"No, I can't explain it, but I can tell you what happened to you, or at least what is supposed to have happened to you. Please sit down, Peter," implored Jane.

"What are you trying to tell me?" Peter asked, now very concerned at her tone.

"There is no easy way to say this," Jane began, tears rolling down her cheeks as she tenderly held Peter's hand. "You're supposed to be dead. You were killed in a road accident on the A580 that day. I'm really sorry, but you're supposed to be dead," she sobbed.

"No! You're mistaken! I'm here, aren't I? There must have been a terrible misunderstanding," protested a disbelieving Peter Stanton. He couldn't believe what he was being told; he couldn't bear to hear what was being said.

"I'm sorry, Dad, but it's true," Josh added. "We all went to your funeral and we saw your body. You were killed. Think about it: I'm twelve years old; Liverpool are playing in the 2005 Champions League Final; and where's your car?" Josh hugged his dad tightly, tears streaming down his face. "Dad, I'm so sorry," he cried. "I love you, Dad. I remember you always. I remember you every day I live. Everything I do and think is in your memory.

In the background, the Champions League Final had reached extra time and beyond and was heading fast towards penalties. There had been near misses at both ends, but no further goals. It remained AC Milan 3, Liverpool 3, but by now no-one in the room was taking much notice as a horrified Peter Stanton began to process the horrifying truth. But there was still a mystery as to how he had managed to be here on this night when he was supposed to be dead.

Peter looked down at his arm and noticed the smart-watch showing a different number in the middle circle. "That's funny," he remarked. "The figure on my watch is saying 30, it was 110 an hour and a half ago."

Both Josh and his mother were mystified and remarked in unison, "What watch?"

They couldn't see any watch on Peter's arm as it was only visible to the wearer. Peter was puzzled and mystified that they couldn't see it, nor could he understand the significance of the number in the circle and its reduction. He had yet to realise that it was the number of minutes he had left alive before being returned to imminent death. He hadn't realised his watch was counting down to the end of his own life, and when 0 was reached, the watch would send him back to where history had unfortunately decreed he had died. The watch would then shatter into a thousand pieces, to devoid detection at the end of its life. It was only operating on a residual current of electrical activity, but enough, just enough, to execute its final task.

The smart-watch was also to emit a sharp electronic hypnotising pulse which would serve to erase Josh and Jane's short-term memory; it would be like this had never happened. There would be no recollection, just something like strange gut feelings in its place; it had to be this way!

The Champions League Final had finished in a 3-3 draw, so it had now reached penalties. Josh, his mum Jane, and dad Peter, were huddled together in an emotional embrace as the penalty shootout began.

Milan went first and missed; Liverpool scored through Hamann; then Pirlo missed for Milan; Liverpool scored again through Cisse. So far, so brilliant for Liverpool, as it was Milan 0, Liverpool 2 on penalties. Could Josh and Peter dare to dream that Liverpool would win the Champions League? They could almost taste the glory.

Then Milan scored their 3rd penalty, while Risse had his penalty saved. It was now 2-1 to Liverpool, and Milan again scored with their 4th penalty through Kaka. The pressure was on Smicer, but he rose to the challenge and made it AC Milan 2, Liverpool 3 on penalties. Milan's Shevchenko had to score or it was all over...

To the unadulterated delight of everybody of the red persuasion, goalkeeper Jerzy Dudek saved Shevchenko's penalty! It was all over: Liverpool had won the Champions League!

In that glorious instant, Josh Stanton and his mother, and most especially his dad, Peter Stanton, went absolutely crazy with delight. It was a glorious instant but was immediately tempered by Peter's remark that his watch was now showing 5! Just five minutes stood between Mr Stanton and oblivion, but he had enjoyed watching possibly Liverpool's finest hour as a sort of miraculous compensation. An extraordinary gift had been bestowed upon him, and Peter Stanton was overjoyed and grateful for what he had just witnessed.

He now realised the importance of the number on his watch; it was down to 4.

"My watch is showing 4," he told his wife and son. "I'm guessing when it reaches zero, it's not going to be good news." His voice cracked and he began to cry. "I don't want to die! I'm too young to die! I love you, Josh, and I love you, Jane, with all my heart!"

"We love you, too. We will always love you and honour you. You will always be my true love and have a very special place in my heart," Jane cried almost hysterical now. "I will never ever forget you, I love you so much."

"I love you, Dad," sobbed Josh. "I love you so much. I have and will miss you so greatly. Please don't go, Dad, please don't go. I love you so much, don't go," he pleaded.

Peter was scared about his impending demise. He was terrified but summoned up the strength to beckon Josh and his mother over for an intense group embrace as his smart-watch showed 1.

He was in the last minute of his specially extended but temporary existence when the watch gave off its foreboding flashes of green. As it counted down to its grim initiation, Josh and his parents embraced as tightly as they could manage and then... Peter Stanton had gone. This time for good.

The smart-watch emitted its electronic hypnotic pulse on its exit, leaving Josh and his mother nonplussed as they stood in the middle of their room embracing tightly. They couldn't understand why they were like that, but on the television Liverpool were parading the Champions League trophy on the pitch in manic celebrations. So what the heck? Why not embrace and celebrate!

It had been a truly extraordinary evening in every sense. Back in 1998, Mr Peter Stanton had unfortunately met his demise and the smart-watch had broken up into a thousand pieces, but its evidence wasn't to be seen anywhere near the A580. The last tantalising aspect of Gabriella Richardson's programming of the smart-watch was manifest as Mr Xavier Richardson perused the abnormal amount of debris in his back garden which had appeared all of a sudden. What would he make of all the debris? Who knows? But one thing is for sure, and that is time, as well as love, moves in most mysterious ways!

The End

Lightning Source UK Ltd.
Milton Keynes UK
UKHW040407051218
333470UK00001B/14/P

9 781786 234087